TO YI,

IT WAS AN HONOUR TO MEET SUCH A NICE GIRL AS YOU, ESPECIALLY ONE WHO LOOKS SO CUTE IN GLASSES

—BEN VANEIJK
2020

Fallen World

by

Ben van Eijk

BEN VAN EIJK

Contents

Prelude 3
Chapter 1 6
Chapter 2 18
Chapter 3 30
Chapter 4 44
Chapter 5 58
Chapter 6 70
Chapter 7 86
Chapter 8 98
Chapter 9 118
Chapter 10 128
Chapter 11 146
Chapter 12 162
Chapter 13 178
Chapter 14 194

FALLEN WORLD

Prelude

A loud crash echoed across a mountainous landscape as a large object flew into the rocks at unfathomable speed. The body-shaped object straightened up with little indication it had just performed a deceleration that would reduce most people to paste. It stood — a white man.

His grey beard was one foot long and thinned out into a braid at the end. He was wearing a leather outfit with many buckles and straps containing jewellery of every kind — some just dull rocks, some exquisite and multi-coloured. Some of the rocks were of a blue so pure they looked almost two-dimensional; only the slightest shadow revealed their third dimension. Surprisingly, none of the jewellery had taken damage after being hurled into the side of a mountain.

The man hunched over suddenly and his whole body twitched slightly as he tensed his muscles, causing two wings to spring from his back. The wings were white-hot tentacles of plasma, as thick as an arm and increasing in size towards the wing's apex. Another object crashed into the winged man, pushing them both flat against the crater of his previous impact.

A woman had just collided with the winged man. She placed her foot on his chest. Her hands doubled in size and turned a shiny grey metal texture, then clamped on to his wings. She pushed his body down with her foot while ripping the wings from his back with her huge metallic hands, screaming sadistically as she did so.

Her long brown hair flicked back and revealed her face; she was rather attractive with a small, hooked nose. Her eyes were quite big and she had small, pouted lips — although right now, she was snarling. Black luminescent fluid spewed from the tear where the man's wings had been torn asunder. The bearded man began laughing as the black fluid spewing from his wounds began reshaping into another version of him, and then another, and then more until the woman was surrounded by bearded men, all of them laughing. The one she was pinning to the ground with her foot fell limp, and she turned around just in time to defend herself from one of the men as he slammed into her. The woman picked herself up, quick as lightning, also showing an affinity for indifference to high speed collisions.

The female's long red cloak flapped in the wind as she quickly ascended to avoid the twenty bearded men flying towards her. Some began firing beams at her, but she was too quick and could easily dodge the white-hot rays of plasma as they flew past her. As the bearded men below fired ineffectual beams her left arm began transforming into a pure black tentacle, extending so far the other end could not be seen. She held the tentacle out straight and began spinning around, faster and faster until just a low buzzing could be heard. She started to angle her body horizontally. The tentacle was now acting like a propeller; it started grinding the top off a nearby mountain. Rocks, trees and chunks of mountain began flying in all directions as it took pieces of mountain away, layer by layer. The woman became more and more horizontal, her tentacle cutting deeper into the mountains as it became increasingly vertical. All the bearded men began flying away from the oncoming destruction; all of them failed to escape. They were instantly churned back into the black fluid from which they were born. An entire mountain range was torn up by the spinning tentacle while clouds above were expelled from the atmosphere by the wind.

One bearded man remained, standing inside the huge canyon left in the spinning tentacle's wake while stones and dirt were still falling toward him from all sides. The woman slowed her spinning when she saw him, and cursed. As she was decelerating, she suddenly felt his arm around her neck. He had snuck up from behind.

FALLEN WORLD

He hissed into her ear.

"You know you won't kill me, and I won't kill you. Why —" The woman's elbow morphed into a giant spike and went straight through the bearded man's stomach. The end became hook shaped, and she began to pull it back to cause even more damage, but the man split in two at her point of penetration. His two halves were now each growing into two more clones of the bearded man.

"Look how much difference you make! We destroy universes just by taking a step — stop this futile activity!" said both bearded men simultaneously. One grew a set of white wings, while the other sprouted black ones. The woman held both arms out, pure blue plasma columns spewing from her hands, luminescent beads splitting off like a viscous fluid as they collided with the bearded men.

***

Chapter 1

The young man suddenly jerked his whole body before it went limp from nearly falling asleep while standing up. He had gotten little sleep the previous night (for the last six years) and the circles under his eyes were already permanent at the age of twenty-two. His sudden movement caught the attention of a few other people in the crowd; those who knew him had a small grin on their faces, comprehending his small spasm. He had managed to catch himself, but due to the nature of the speech being given in front of the entire population of the city, it was sure to happen a few more times.

Every year the city of Swevender underwent a magical ritual consisting of three major spells. The people of the city believed it was to keep them from floating into the great abyss. Such a belief stemmed from ignorance, but it is not the people's fault; they had no way of learning the truth about the world in which they were living. Swevender was actually a gigantic floating city, artificially created, and thousands of years old. The entire city was made from 1,943 segments and each segment was made from a porous concrete. The top part of a segment on which the residents walk and live was typically a flat crescent of grass, or sometimes in the form of a rounded pyramid. The underside of each segment ended in a tapering point five metres beneath the surface.

When Swevender was being constructed, enchanted and assembled, each segment was filled in with nutrient rich soil or water. Now a simple cycle of evaporation, precipitation and maintenance sustained the Swevender inhabitants. Where there are no buildings, the city was covered in thick vegetation and crystal-clear waters.

FALLEN WORLD

The city was constructed and raised by three powerful conjurers, thousands of years ago. Io was the youngest of the three and was worshipped for his creativity and unceasing productivity, be it art or labour — he was never standing still. The spell of Io concerned the accumulation of water vapour. It kept a cloud just beneath, and constantly within reach of, the city. Swevender used water in many different ways to support itself. It was the city's main energy source, and many citizens were adept in the art of 'water wielding', a technique from the three conjurers that had been maintained throughout the lifetime of Swevender.

Kern was the genius of the three, recognised for his diplomacy and brilliant mathematical abilities. He was the one to sew together the complicated puzzle of the 1,943 pieces of Swevender into a wonderful self-sustaining masterpiece.

The last of the three was Marsa. Marsa was known for her compassion and strength. It was said that she could have easily destroyed the other two magic wielders. While all three wizards were regarded as the most powerful in their entire history, Marsa's spell was what held the city up. Only someone with a great abundance of power could cast a spell to hold so much weight for years on end.

Swevender had roughly three thousand citizens. The city achieved perfect balance due to its complex yet efficient design. About twenty percent of the city's segments were dedicated purely to farmland. Most people grew their own food and livestock. Some houses would pool their resources and have a small farm between multiple families. The farmland was maintained easily, as the soil was rich in nutrients and rain occurred in ample amounts on a regular basis. The entire city of Swevender had a thick cloud layer just beneath it; the lifeblood of the city. During the creation of the city, the three magic wielders, Io, Kern and Marsa taught the people of Swevender how to wield water and exploit its almost endless energy. They spoke of how everything is made up of smaller particles, and how each particle is sacred; if one was to be destroyed it would release infinite energy, destroying everything.

The citizens believed water contained the highest level of energy and, unlike every other kind of matter, that its wielding held no risk of destroying the universe. Water was easily accessible, as the permanent layer of clouds cradling the city thanks to Io's spell provided more than enough water to supply any magical needs. Any excess water in the soil evaporated into the cumulus nimbus attached to the bottom of Swevender, thus continuing the cycle that helped it flourish.

The clouds extended about one kilometre beyond the radius of the city, obscuring the residents' vision of what could lie beneath their city. To the residents of Swevender, they were floating on an endless sea of fog and anything that fell over the edge of the city was lost forever: nothing lived out there. There was no fate worse than falling over the city's edge. The body would be lost forever, and the person's essence would never become part of the city, providing nutrients and perpetuating the cycle, contributing even in death.

Swevender had a tight knit community, since their whole world was the three thousand people in the city. Connections between people were valued highly and rumours travelled fast. If people had problems with each other, they generally worked out a solution involving the two being kept together, encouraged by the philosophy of the three water wielders from so long ago.

The young man attempting to stay awake during the yearly speech was someone without a single one of these connections.

He became a self-styled rebel at a young age and seemed to be stuck in that phase still. He always had something important to do — he didn't know what, exactly, but it was forever urgent and prevented him from fulfilling other obligations. He was quite smart, but disappointed many people around him by wasting his mind and (admittedly excessive) energy on trivial pursuits. This was clearly evidenced by the inside of his house: neglected and half-finished gadgets were scattered everywhere. His garden had three humongous trees, planted by one of the previous owners of this segment, which he allowed to grow forty metres high. There were small rope bands around the trees' branches, providing places for bromeliads to plant their roots and suck moisture from the air. A few small ponds lay between the trees. All of them had a green surface of algae and were mainly used to provide a bit of humidity to the surrounding trees and plants.

Despite the untidy look of the garden, it was actually well maintained. The sleepy young man loved to garden and found it one the few things he could do at an easy pace without rushing himself to finish; since it had no end it couldn't be rushed. The garden was like a small rainforest with a canopy in the middle where the three trees overlapped, blocking out ninety percent of the sun.

The young man's name was Seth Cost. He liked the peace of mind provided from being surrounded by plants, finding inspiration for other projects. He also had an immaculately maintained vegetable garden since eating was one of his passions and he refused to compromise in this matter. Despite his love for food and eating, he was still a rather skinny guy and would always get comments on how thin he was. His long limbs didn't help decrease the attention he got in this matter either, although soon after meeting him most people were too distracted by his inability to listen and his direct manner to comment on his appearance.

Seth saw himself as honest, merely speaking his mind — which was true to a certain extent, but most other people saw it as being rude and blunt. Seth also tended to ignore someone's offense at his remarks, just seeing it as a hindrance to the conversation. He had dark brown dreadlocks hanging just past his shoulders, well maintained sweet smelling. He had a pale complexion and his nose was a little more bulbous than most. His eyebrows were quite thick and gave the initial impression that he was up to no good, although some saw it as a nice frame for his piercing green eyes. He could not grow a full beard and the whiteness of his facial hair made it practically translucent. His favourite outfit was a dark blue robe over loose clothes with as many pockets as possible. This allowed Seth to always be over prepared for any situation, stuffing his pockets with things that *maybe* had the *potential* to be useful.

Listening to the droning speech, Seth shook his head sharply to stay focussed, while the head of Swevender University orchestrated the annual ritual. Each year, three of the best students of water wielding were chosen to help perform the ritual. This year, Seth, Kurt Scutt and Stacey Linster were chosen. Kurt was another pale young lad, with jet black hair combed to one side, and a weak chin. Most of his features were quite small, giving his face an even paler look as his cheeks and forehead dominated his features. Kurt was chosen as his family was one of the oldest and most influential in Swevender, occupying five percent of the city's segments.

Seth was amazed he had been chosen this year. His theory was that one of his teachers saw some potential in him and believed he would show more motivation and focus if given some responsibility. Seth was more enthused that someone was thinking of him at all. He always assumed he was passing just under the radar, but now he was casting Io's spell — someone had definitely been paying attention to know Io was the wizard he most identified with.

Stacey Linster was going to be casting the spell of Marsa. She resembled the female water wielder's statue quite closely: a heart-shaped face with a gently pointed chin and nose. She had freckles dotting her cheeks and nose and was almost always smiling. Long lashes hid most of her eyes, but what peeked through was shining with energy. This left the spell of Kern for Kurt, a coincidental similarity of names he had found very appropriate.

The ritual was always followed by a celebration. The celebration was also practical in that it was used to consume any excess food and water that had been collected throughout the year, helping keep the balance maintained by Swevender for thousands of years. The euphoria in the air always caused people to act intoxicated — although the alcohol also helped. Every year there was drama that would be spoken about for weeks afterwards. This year, Seth was predicting it would involve him punching Kurt in his stupid face. Seth had been regarded as the most gifted student in his water wielding class, gaining admiration from his fellow students — until Kurt Scutt transferred into the class.

Once Kurt arrived, Seth was forgotten. Kurt, being of the famous Scutt family, gained admiration for just being born, it seemed to Seth. Although he shunned attention when he got it, deep down Seth actually enjoyed it. His regard for Kurt was lessened further still, since he had heard Kurt was only allowed into the water wielding class due to his inheritance, not his skills or endurance. Seth now silently cursed Kurt, not only for stealing his spotlight in class, but for sneaking his way into participating in the ritual too.

Soon the ritual master would call the three students from the main crowd to step forth and reveal who was casting which spell. Seth felt a gentle tap on his shoulder and turned to see Mrs. Scutt, Kurt's mother. She had the same jet-black hair, long and straight, and skin even paler than her son's. Her eyes were a dark brown that was almost black. She had such a serious face that when she smiled, everyone smiled with her; her whole face changed, dismissing any negative feelings someone might have had about her. It was hard to believe she was Kurt's mother, since she was about half his height and – Seth thought – *much* more pleasant to talk to.

"Have you prepared everything?" she asked Seth with genuine concern.

"Of course, I was ready a few days ago. I read the scroll a few times last night to practice, but it should be fine," Seth answered, a little directly, suspecting she was one of the many people who believed he was incompetent. She smiled, mistaking his tone for friendly.

"It's going to be a nice ritual this year I think, this year's class has turned out some great water wielders."

Seth was a little disarmed by her friendliness and determined to respond more amicably.

"Yeah, I think so too. This ritual will make next year's celebration bigger than ever."

Seth looked at Mrs Scutt and let his eyes wander over her body. Seth thought she had maintained herself quite well over the years; he could see himself trying more than one stupid thing at the celebration tonight. He wasn't usually someone who pursued older women, but the bonus of irritating Kurt made her look even more attractive.

"I probably could have left the ritual scroll at home. I know the whole thing backwards." Seth laughed a little as he bragged to Mrs. Scutt, wishing he knew her first name. His smile suddenly disappeared as he realised that he had indeed left the scroll at home.

He looked a little guiltily at Mrs. Scutt and excused himself.

"Sorry, I have to go grab something."

"Don't tell me you forgot the sacred water!" Mrs. Scutt was almost laughing.

Seth pulled out his vial with water blooming with algae.

"No, of course not, but it turns out I actually *did* leave the scroll at home." He turned to run but she grabbed his arm and pulled the water vial from his hand. She inspected the scum-covered water.

"What did you do with your sacred water?" She asked Seth, looking skeptically at the vial. He began inching slowly away, eager to retrieve the scroll before he was called before the crowd to recite Io's spell.

"Nothing, it's still sacred — in fact, algae makes it more sacred!"
Mrs Scutt laughed again.

"Uh, sure, but you are *supposed* to *remove* the algae... Look, you go get your scroll and I will go get a vial of sacred water. Kurt had a few extra ones made in case something like this happened."

"Don't need it, water's fine!" Seth said quite loudly, the distance between them increasing. She was still holding the vial, scrutinising it once again.

"Don't worry, you get the scroll, I'll get the water, I live closer than you, it's no problem."
Seth really didn't have time to argue anymore. He shouted "thank you" towards Mrs. Scutt, catching the attention of the head of the University. Seth gave him a thumbs up in response to his puzzled look, and sped homewards.

***

The two winged men held out their hands, directing the blue plasma energy flow towards each other to form a triangle.

"Well this just looks cool! See, we can *work together to make something beautiful!" The bearded men shouted, voices in synch. The woman screamed, the pulsating beams shooting out of her hands growing thicker in diameter.*

"Would you just shut your stupid mouth!"

The two men were pushed back by the beams until they couldn't be seen anymore. The woman stopped firing her blue plasma and began searching the area with darting glances. She knew he wasn't dead, but they were both at the point of giving up. They would soon either vanish for a while until they inevitably ran into each other again or stop and talk. The latter almost always ended in more fighting, so she hoped he would just disappear.

Far off in the distance, she saw one of the mountains rising from the ground, and knew it wasn't over quite yet. The mountain disappeared into the clouds, another following, and then nothing. The clouds above her began to open with unnatural speed. Just as quick, a familiar looking mountain appeared above her. As it started to get closer, the female's body turned into liquid, then vapour; it twisted across the surface of the mountain now thundering towards the ground. The vapour easily slid around the mountain and avoided being crushed. The vapour began to retake the form of the cloaked woman, becoming liquid and then solid.
The second mountain came down on top of her even faster than the last one, but she was prepared; she had already created a solid wall of metal above her, blocking the mountain's descent.

The force of the flying mountain was easy for her to hold back, but then something else as big as a mountain hit her gigantic metal shield, and another. Gigantic chunks of moon were raining down on her metal shield, each piece shattering and spilling over the sides. The bombardment pushed her closer and closer to the ground until she was hovering only metres away from it. Her shield was cutting off her visibility, inviting surprise attacks. But if she couldn't see the bearded men, then they couldn't see her either... she let the huge shield drift to the ground. Celestial matter continued bombarding it, bending it inwards. Before she was crushed under her metal shield, she pointed her open palm

FALLEN WORLD

at the ground in front of her and it disintegrated, forming the mouth of a tunnel. She flew into it with her hand extended, pushing more dirt and rock out of the way as she did so.

She could travel swiftly like this and was already well out of harm's way as more bits of moon rained from the clouds. The cloaked woman ended her subterranean journey and emerged from the ground unnoticed. She waited, patiently hovering at a safe distance, watching the humongous chunks of rock flatten her metal shield even further and compact the dirt beneath it with kilotons of force. It was quite a sight to see — but she had seen grander things than a moon being taken apart piece by piece and hurled into a mountain valley. Still this was an exceptional scene. Eventually the bombardment stopped — or maybe there was no more moon left for the bearded men to throw. She saw a black dot descend from the clouds. She began flying towards him at a speed, but the second bearded man came down on top of her, elbow first. She shouted in surprise as the first man flew in to help push her down even faster. Suddenly from all over her body, metal spikes extended outward with lightning speed, impaling both bearded men. A shower of blood erupted from both men and the spikes became molten inside them.
They screamed as metal coated their insides and poured back out through melted holes in their flesh. The two men began to fall from the air, a glowing viscous liquid spewing from their bodies. While falling, one of the men lifted his hand and a piece of liquid metal starting dripping upwards out of a hole in his palm. The stream then grew into a gooey column of molten liquid aimed directly at the cloaked woman hanging in the air above him. She reacted quickly and fired an even larger beam of white-hot energy back at him, pushing the molten liquid aside and bathing the bearded men in pure plasma. The white beam hit the ground and a humongous shockwave expanded from its centre, travelling so fast it cut straight through a range of mountains

without hesitation. The shockwave didn't show any sign of slowing when it disappeared over the horizon.

The woman was panting now. She knew it was finished. The bearded man had been melted and then completely incinerated. He could still come back, she knew, but it would be a long time before she would see him again.

The rumble of the shockwave echoed across the now barren landscape. Their fight had destroyed everything; a huge layer of the ground had been ripped up, exposing the bed rock. The rock was hot to the touch and had exploded where super-heated pockets of air had expanded. All that could be seen was rubble, smoke coming from small cracks extending across the landscape. The desolate scene continued to tremble as the shockwave made its slow journey across the surface of the planet.

FALLEN WORLD

Chapter 2

Seth was already panting during his short run; by the time he reached his front door, he was ready to collapse. Seth opened the door and searched around frantically for the scroll. His desk — originally his workspace — had slowly turned into a storage area as more and more clutter began occupying the surface. Once he was certain the scroll was not among that mess, he turned to scan the room. Then he heard a low rumble, getting louder quickly, and the room around him started to shake.

Pot plants began falling off shelves, smashing as they hit the floor and scattering dirt and stones across the ground. *They must have started the ritual already*, Seth thought. He started to sweat as anxiety combined with his physical exertions. He placed his robe on the chair by his desk to cool down a little — and noticed the scroll sticking out of his pocket.

"You have got to be kidding me!" Seth slapped his forehead in disbelief.

He quickly picked up his robe, grabbed the scroll, and tucked his robe under his arm, still warm from his sudden burst of activity. He ran out the door and noticed something odd; things had changed, but he wasn't sure what. He turned and ran towards the central segment, where the ritual was already beginning. Seth stopped himself just in time; there appeared to be a gap of three metres between his segment and his neighbour's.

He flailed his arm frantically trying to stop himself going over the edge. He stretched out his hand holding the scroll and a panicked burst of water went flying down towards the cloud beneath him. It made a hole in the cloud and he thought he saw the brown colour of soil through the gap, but more water vapour quickly crept back to fill the breach, blocking his vision. The kickback from firing his pulse of water pushed him back onto safe ground, stopping Seth from being lost to the abyss… which was apparently the same colour as soil?

Seth was cursing in surprise. He had almost died in the worst way imaginable, and now he realised he was slowly floating away from the rest of the city. He ran to the other side of his plot and saw other segments slowly detaching from the main bulk of Swevender. He could try a bit of water wielding to help him leap from one segment to the next until he was back in the centre, but the distance already looked nearly impossible to jump. Seth had at one time taught himself to create a propellor of water he used to hover several metres above the ground. In an effort to outshine Kurt, he had flown well outside the border of Swevender to show off to his classmates. Seth's impetuosity led him to fly a little too far where the cloud was too thin to provide sufficient water for a propellor and almost fell to his death. The cloud between him and his neighbouring segment already looked much thinner now but, memory multiplying his fear, he ran towards the edge anyway. He moved with the thought of gaining enough momentum to fling himself across, assisted by his propellor, but he skidded to a halt inches away from the edge, too scared he might actually fall to his death this time.

Shouting was coming from the direction of the central segment. Seth tried shouting too, but so many voices at once just became a muddled noise. The situation needed no further deduction. It was clear: Swevender was falling to pieces. Seth thought he could bind his piece back towards the centre using the spell on his scroll, but now he noticed that the scroll was gone, most likely shot through the clouds along with the water burst that had spared him from the abyss. He could see the underside of Swevender's segments through the fog of its cloud foundation now, and was fascinated. They looked like lots of small, concrete hills, all ending in a rounded peak. It was a sight that had been only metres beneath him for his whole life, but still, he had never seen it, never *thought* about it.

The sight of the bottom of the other segments alerted Seth to the fact that he was sinking. His panic rose as the cloud and other segments were suddenly swept away from him by an invisible force. He could see the ground now; the abyss was shades of brown and grey, coming towards him slowly as he continued sinking. Seth looked up and saw the circular central segment of Swevender, the only piece of the city without any corners, still higher than any other segment. Seth surmised they had already cast the levitation spell, so the central segment would be safe from sinking. But *he* was supposed to cast the cloud cover spell, the spell that provided the source of energy for all other magic in Swevender. What would everyone do now?

Seth noticed water vapour begin to accumulate beneath the central segment. *Of course — a lot of people know how to cast Io's spell from other rituals*, Seth thought, feeling a little relieved the only person he had to worry about now was himself. He looked down again, knowing that soon the entire city and population of Swevender would just be a cloud to him, but he needed to focus on solving his sinking problem. The great brown and grey abyss was getting awfully close, and he couldn't see any other segments in the distance now.

Seth scanned the approaching landscape around him for anything other than what he now assumed was dirt and rock. He noticed a tall figure in the distance walking towards his descending segment. Its movement was very halted and awkward. Seth held up both of his hands as if clutching an invisible staff. Water flew out of the ponds in his small garden, eager to fulfil the idea of the shape Seth envisioned in his hands. He held the shaft of water up to his eye, using it as a telescope. The water had been bent into the shape of a lens inside the scope and allowed Seth to see this creature more clearly. Green particles of algae floated lazily across the lens of his liquid telescope.

FALLEN WORLD

The creature's head was about forty percent of its whole body. Its eyes were as big as fists and its mouth was hanging open, dribbling an excessive amount of silvery fluid to the ground. It had extremely skinny limbs for something with such bulk. Its massive elephantine feet dragged slowly, pushing dirt aside while its long gangly legs lazily shuffled forward. It left four massive trails in its wake, its huge knuckles also scraping across the dirt. The skin of the creature seemed to be made of dirt too, with bits constantly cracking and repairing themselves all over its body.

Above him, Seth could see the central segment floating away, now surrounded by a huge cloud as other segments trailed behind. Seth remembered seeing a few lines of Stacey's scroll and was desperately trying to remember the rest when he saw one of the other segments sinking towards the creature. Seth stood motionless while he watched the creature raise its hand in a swinging motion and bat the segment away with one of its gigantic hands. The segment split in half where the massive hand had violently struck it. Both halves hit the ground at speed, sending rubble flying at all angles until they skidded to a halt in the distance.

Seth's segment hit the ground with a thump and a totter, he heard the mess inside slide across his floor and collide with the wall. Steadying himself, Seth ran to the edge of his segment. It was now angled so that the ground on which it had landed was *just* within reach, if he stretched. He poked the ground with his foot, confirming it was solid, then stepped slowly onto it. The monster was only a hundred metres away from him now and was holding a piece of concrete from the segment it had just decimated. The monster swung its arm towards Seth, releasing the makeshift projectile to send it flying towards him. Seth stumbled backwards in trepidation, losing his footing. As he was falling, Seth's surroundings suddenly went out of focus.

It didn't get darker, like he was losing consciousness — it just *changed*. When he hit the ground, he felt grass beneath him. Strange — the only grass he remembered being in the vicinity was on his small segment of Swevender. But there was no longer any evidence of his home, and he was surrounded by what appeared to be graves.

He heard a high-pitched nasal voice behind him.

"It's about time you fell here."

He turned to see a slight, humanoid creature, with bright red skin. It had small horns sticking from its head above two glowing orange eyes and an ear-to-ear smile revealing a set of razor-sharp teeth. It looked like a skeleton wrapped in red skin, its anatomy unobscured and similar to a human's. It spoke again.

"Are you alright?" it asked, with genuine concern in its voice.

"Uuuhh yeah, I think so… where am I?" Seth was looking around now. He appeared to be inside a translucent dome, about fifty metres in diameter. The surface of the dome was constantly rippling, making it impossible to focus on what was going on outside. But 'outside' was hard to judge too; the scenery seemed to change to a completely different location every second. One moment Seth could see a desert infested with giant snakes that could swallow Seth's house whole. The next second there was a dark landscape illuminated only by strobing flashes of lightning, revealing a completely metallic world with trees made of smooth, flawless metal.

Seth was completely in awe. He barely had enough time to absorb what was happening in each world. The next scene was completely made of a strange organic material, with structures made of dripping viscera. He thought he saw a being shuffling along, made of the same weird substance — but then it all changed into a barren, underwater world with small lights in the distance.

Inside their bubble, the light was constantly changing as different suns shone through its dancing surface. The graves surrounding them all seemed to be extremely intricate. Some were twice as tall as Seth, and the constantly changing light sometimes gave the impression that the grave's surfaces were moving. There was also a large statue in the middle that stood out for some reason... — its surface didn't reflect light the same way the surrounding stone did. The statue portrayed two cloaked people in dramatic poses: a tall woman with a long braid hanging past her waist and a handsome man with slicked back hair.

The small imp creature raised both its arms in a welcoming gesture.

"This, young man, is the Restyard."

It perched on small grave to keep him roughly eye level with Seth, who was now standing up and rubbing his bruised backside.

"That doesn't really explain where I am. A second ago there was some... *thing* trying to kill me, and my home was literally falling from the sky, and now I'm inside this rippling bubbly joogle!"

"Ah yes, I guess I should explain things or you'll keep pestering me with questions for the next year." The imp grinned, his pointed teeth making Seth slightly uncomfortable. Seth's eyes widened in surprise.

"For the next year? I have to go back" he exclaimed. The imp's grin disappeared.

"I'm afraid that will prove to be quite impossible for you, lad. You're in the Restyard now." It raised its hands again, indicating the current surroundings. Seth sighed as he realised he should start making his questions more direct.

"What is 'the Restyard' then? It looks like a graveyard to me."

"It would be a graveyard if anyone here was dead, but we are all very much alive. Believe me, if we *could* die, we would be dead. But then, I wouldn't be here to help you," replied the imp.

"You see, we are failed familiars. Our masters created us, but then improved their skills — as someone who constantly practises should, of course. But they learned how to make more powerful and efficient familiars, so we were made obsolete and banished to spend the remainder of our 'lives' here."

Seth looked thoughtfully at the ground.

"So all these graves are occupied by living people? They can hear me talking now?"

"No, most cannot. It's possible Old Five Ears can, but he sleeps in an open casket. He likes to watch the sky." The imp pointed to a square hole bordered with stone bricks.

"Most of us have seen everything happen a million times over, said the same words in every different combination, have been known by every name, and never encounter anything new. As you get older you realise everything — *everything* — repeats itself, and being alive to constantly rewatch it all is *torture*."

Seth held his hand out in a stopping gesture.

"Wait, wait, before you tell me any more: who are you? And could you please let me out of here?"

"Oh, apologies. I am Red. Like I said, I have been known by many names, so now we just use descriptive terms to avoid confusion." The small imp pressed his hands together and bowed politely.

"And you are?"

Seth held his hand out to shake the small imp's hand as he introduced himself.

"I am Seth Cost. It's good to meet you, especially since you seem to have saved me from death by flying rock!" Seth peeked back over his shoulder and now saw a grey, mountainous landscape saturated with rain. As his glance returned to Red, he saw the imp inspecting Seth's hand curiously.

FALLEN WORLD

"This is a custom I am not familiar with, but ok..." The imp held his hand out in a similar fashion to Seth. Seth reached for his hand and tried to shake it, but shaking Red's hand was like pushing a house. Seth brought his hand back to his side, momentarily timid.

He continued his enquiry:

"So why is there no rock or monster behind me now?"

Red held up his hand in a stopping motion.

"As I was saying, everything repeats itself — just like the destruction of your city. It was inevitable; the element binders who destroyed it have done so millions of times. We are all sick of seeing it over and over again. So, we are trying to achieve the closest thing to death possible, using a sort of meditation to clear our minds. We are depriving our senses to achieve a state of zen, and bury ourselves deep underground to avoid being disturbed. Believe me, if I could leave here, I would do it in a flash, but the element binders who placed us here were very skilled and we do not have the power to overcome their spell. You shouldn't be able to enter here either — people normally encounter an unseen wall, but the recent shockwave that has disturbed so much of your planet must have weakened the spell."

Seth was amazed how much the creature knew about his own world. He couldn't even begin to figure out how to get back there, and he'd only taken a few steps on "his" planet before arriving here in the Restyard. Red spoke with ease as he continued his explanation.

"The Restyard travels through different universes almost every second, making it almost impossible to find and even harder to break into — or out of. We are all creatures of pure magic, so we can never exit, but *you* can, at any time. This is a failsafe the element binders created, but the chances are you will end up somewhere completely alien to you. Luckily for you, I have lived above ground here so long that I know the sequence of universe shifts off by heart. I know that it will be roughly one of your years before the cycle brings us to your world again.

"You see, I witness a second of your universe every year, and I have been following hundreds of thousands of stories in this same manner. I saw your city being created and I saw how it almost fell. Over the course of five years, I watched the shockwave of energy that damaged it — quite fast actually, considering it was 856 years before you arrived here. I am glad to have someone in here to talk with again, however you're not our first visitor. This bubble has a specific sequence for where and when it jumps so its creators can find it again, but it is not meant to be found by anybody else."
Red the imp began rubbing his hands together and his demeanour picked up a little as he began the next part of his well-rehearsed story.
"The pair of element binders have hidden us away here because we know their secrets. We have all been the right hand to one of the two at some point and have the potential to shift the balance of power out of their favour, which is why I am going to use the next year passing these secrets onto you; I'm not exactly happy about being sentenced to immortality inside this bubble."

"Forgive me, but I don't see any food here. How exactly am I going to last a whole year?" Seth was suddenly angry with uncertainty.
"That will be your first lesson. I know the element binders taught your people element binding, but they misled you when they said water was the only safe source of energy. I know how to create food from virtually nothing — even the water in your body is more than enough to flood this entire chamber." The imp pointed an open palm to the ground and an apple tree grew in a matter of seconds, its branches heavy with fruit.

Seth was impressed by Red's display of power and began to listen to his story a little more cooperatively. The imp lowered his hand and an apple drifted slowly from the tree into his open palm. He sank razor sharp teeth into the freshly grown fruit with a loud crunch. The imp continued to speak with a mouthful of apple.

"Thif if why oo eed my helf." He swallowed a bit of apple and added "young man."

"How did you do that?" Seth looked at the tree in amazement. Red pointed at a stain on Seth's robe.

"Any food you spilled on your robe and failed to wash can be used to make any form of the food. I could have made an apple sauce tree — would have made a mess but still very possible. If you spilled any steak on there, we can have a good meal right now!" proclaimed Red proudly.

"Yeah probably, but I don't know which stain is what, and I'm afraid we might make something neither of us want to eat." Seth blushed, a little bit embarrassed.

"Well, the point I am trying to make is this: *any* element can be used as a source of energy, and this greatly influences the outcome of your spell. Until now you have only been using water as a source of energy. Granted, it is an extremely efficient source, but that is more because it comes partially from a different universe —" Red cut himself off.

"— but that's a matter I will not get into right now," said Red casually, knocking Seth off balance with his casual reveal of such revolutionary information.

"Basically, you always fire beams of water because water is where your energy comes from, but imagine you could fire a beam of rock, or fire, or even pure energy! And not just firing a beam; you can create a wieldable sword made of fire, or use your own essence to create another living version of yourself!" Red was getting excited as he explained the potential Seth had been missing all these years.

"Please! Teach me all you have to teach! I'm happy to get started right now then, if I can do this I don't want to waste any time!" Seth responded eagerly.

Red's smile broadened significantly as he rubbed his hands together.

"First things first: jewellery! You are not a real Element Binder without some serious decorations."

FALLEN WORLD

Chapter 3

His year in the bubble was not nearly long enough for him to learn everything Red had to teach, but what he did learn was utterly mind boggling. The first hurdle he had to overcome was acknowledging that the water wielders who created Swevender were not infallible. They had chosen water as a principle source of energy not because it contained more energy than other matter — actually, every kind of matter seemed to contain *limitless* power. Seth had been quite good at water wielding in Swevender. He was powerful and controlled; he could submerge someone in water up to their necks, then with a wave of his hand have them bone dry, with a perfect cube of water next to them. Unlike his classmates he could create a propeller of water large and fast enough to keep him floating steadily above the ground. But his experiments had led to Seth almost dying while practising this water manifestation, flying too close to the edge of Swevender's great cloud stratum. Now, after a year of studying with Red, Seth was able to float using oxygen as his catalyst. He could even use a small amount of water on his skin to create a year's supply of drinking water (a trick that took a long time to master, but even now Seth could still taste himself in the water).

Seth's hands were covered in many rings, at least two per finger, each with its own unique characteristics. This made them easy to distinguish from each other, but reflected its wearer's complete lack of style. No matter: Seth could now manipulate almost any kind of matter, so he made sure he had his favourite ones literally on hand at all times. Red taught him that each type of matter has a different effect. Some were better for certain things than others. Fire was great for casting devastating beams: A ring of flint on his index finger and one of iron on his thumb were able to create the source for fire spells. He kept some magnesium on a ring around his middle finger for creating even hotter flames — and for keeping his garden healthy.

Seth also had a ring with water inside a tiny glass globe, as he was already adept at using this element and felt more comfortable having it with him. On his pinky finger was a ring of gold Red insisted he wear, although Seth hadn't found anything so special about that metal. Too soft. Seth also had one ring encasing a small apple seed, but he didn't want to eat another apple again for years if it could be helped. At least having that with him ensured he would always have *something* to eat.

A lot of the sleeping familiars in the Restyard still had jewellery left over from their days with their master, so Seth had many sources to create his personal trinkets. His fingers were covered in as many variations of matter as possible, while still maintaining the use of his hands. His way to test this was if he was able to drum a nice tune on his legs without feeling encumbered by his jewellery; then he didn't have too many rings.

He was also wearing a chain around his neck, weighted with globes containing different liquids and stones. In the beginning Seth had felt a bit silly decorated this way, but after a few months he forgot he was even wearing the jewellery. His facial hair had darkened slightly over his year in the bubble and now grew a little thicker. He now had what could be called a goatee clinging to his chin, but the rest of his face could have been shaved using a sharp gust of wind.

"Well, it's not often I am sorry to see someone go Seth, but you have taught me a bit in this past year too," Red said tearfully as he was shaking Seth's hand.

"I taught you more, obviously, but it's still very rare for me to learn anything nowadays. I've seen it all already."

Seth was also getting a little emotional. Being in such close proximity with someone for so long is bound to create some sort of bond, regardless of how complementary their personalities are. That said, Seth had found Red to be a suitably appropriate person. He too seemed to be rebelling against something and had the same 'just go with the flow' attitude. Red had taught him more than just element binding (Seth now preferred calling it 'matter manipulation'. He had thought up six different ways to name his powers over the past year); he had also taught him the importance of hard work, sticking to your principles and a good night's sleep. Seth and Red now even shared a few mannerisms after their year in the Restyard together.

Through the glassy surface of the bubble encompassing their tiny world, they had witnessed planets being destroyed and reborn. For Seth it was an extremely interesting distraction, watching worlds flicker past a second at a time. They passed at least thirty cities submerged under the greatest masses of water Seth had ever seen — "oceans", Red called them. Most universes didn't make any sense to Seth; a mass of colours swirling around chaotically, or sometimes just black, so when something coherent came into view, he took note. His favourite sight was spotting people halfway through falling over. The more damage they looked like they would cause, the more entertaining it was for Seth. Red called him puerile the first time he caught Seth laughing at someone else's misfortune, but before the year was out, Red was pointing them out to Seth himself and laughing before Seth had a chance to even see.

"I never thought I would want to stay in such a tiny place as your Restyard, but I do find myself regretting leaving." Seth finished shaking Red's hand and wiped a tear away from his eye with a ring covered hand.

"But I guess it's time to get back to my fight; with everything you taught me, that monster won't stand a chance now. I can't thank you enough, Red."

A bony finger extended from one of Red's outstretched arms to indicate Seth should turn his attention to outside the bubble.

FALLEN WORLD

"Your stop is coming up in a few minutes. Don't forget you were already being assaulted by that creature; you will have to deal with that *as soon* as you are back — no time to stop and reminisce. And solve it in a way I can be proud of; I will be watching it happen for a long time," Red reminded Seth.

"You have no need to worry about me. I'll shatter that thing to pieces in such a spectacular way, you won't want turn away for even a second, once every year."

Seth was now paying close attention to the outside of the bubble to make sure he didn't miss his world in the queue.

Red smiled behind Seth as he held out his hand, palm toward Seth, and said:

"You are going to regret spreading your sense of humour to me in this past year though..."

Seth turned his head to look at Red, asking "why is tha-", but before Seth could finish his sentence, air rippled from Red's hand and Seth burst out of the bubble at an alarming speed. Seth's surroundings were suddenly missing the familiar rippling sky he had grown accustomed to over the past year. He fell to the ground as a rock flew past him, dangerously close. He stood up and wondered how long Red had been laughing while he had been falling to the ground.

Seth stood up and dusted himself off while looking around. He saw the long-armed creature prying another rock from the dirt. Seth raised both arms dramatically, conscious of his audience in the Restyard. Seth had made an arc with his hands, framing the creature where it stood, rock in hand. It pitched the new rock towards Seth, but the rock shattered mid-air and came nowhere near him. The creature cocked its head to the side in confusion, but its expression didn't change. Seth focused on his ring holding a small piece of azurite, and a beam made of bright blue stone shot out at an incredible velocity, growing like the root of a tree. The small stone driving the stone beam had a bright blue colour with small darker blues running across its surface like lightning, giving the stone beam a beautiful appearance despite its intention. The stone pole curved and pierced the creature's head. Seth lowered his hand and the azurite beam fell to the ground, crushing more of the gangly-armed creature under its weight.

Seth looked at the fallen creature with pride and relief but couldn't help thinking that this was actually a little anticlimactic. He had hoped for a longer battle — maybe even a scar — but his enemy already lay defeated on the ground. Seth walked up to the corpse of the beast and saw that its blood was a thick, silvery ooze. There was more and more leaking out from underneath the blue stone he had generated. As he stood over the vanquished beast, he revelled in the growth of his powers. Maybe he should indeed have expected a quick conclusion to this battle; with his powers as they were now it was hard to imagine having trouble with anyone — or any*thing* — else. The ease of his victory felt bittersweet. He didn't want to get hurt but he didn't want to win without a challenge either.

Seth took a sample of the creature's blood to see if he would be able to utilise any of its unique properties in the future. A small glass vial materialised in his hand and scooped up some 'blood'. He remembered that Red was probably watching him. He turned around to where he had exited the bubble and gave a thumbs up and a smile. He lingered a little. He wanted to make sure Red definitely saw it from one of the Restyard's yearly journeys through his universe. His smile disappeared as he heard rock cracking behind him. Seth turned to see the creature's silvery blood dripping *up* the blue stone that had crushed it. A huge crack had appeared in the column, and through it came tendrils of silver ooze, poking at the air.

Quickly the ooze took the shape of one of the creature's lanky arms and began swinging about wildly. It knocked Seth to the ground before he had a chance to react and his vial of ooze flew from his hand, smashing on the ground. A metallic goo reflection of the original beast was now looming above Seth. It raised both its enormous hands together above its head. The huge blob of fist began to fall towards Seth, now lying on the ground. Seth panicked and with a wave of his hand, a blue column erupted from the stone on the ground beneath him, pushing him sideways and out of harm's way. He had cast this last spell a bit carelessly and was now winded; the stone had smashed into his chest. Seth used the dirt beneath him to create a column, elevating himself out of the creature's reach. He stood up, still finding it hard to suck in any air. The creature began to pound at the base of his small dirt podium. It was a surprisingly effective attack; Seth found he had to kneel to stop from falling over. The creature succeeded in breaking Seth's dirt tower and it began to tilt to the ground with Seth still on it.

Whatever the creature is made of, it must be very heavy, thought Seth. *I should definitely get a sample of its essence when I figure out how to beat it.* He jumped and simultaneously summoned another dirt column, landing roughly. This column was three times as wide and therefore much sturdier. He peeked over the edge, now able to breathe somewhat normally, and clicked his fingers. The ensuing spark expanded in less than a second; a fiery pole accelerated downwards and encompassed the entire creature. Seth blasted the beast with fire for about three seconds and looked down, expecting to see a small black pile of ashes. Instead he saw the silver monster still hammering mercilessly against his dirt fort.

Seth shouted in rage at the creature.

"You should be dead!"

Seth manifested a huge blue rock to drop on its head, but even as it fell, Seth realised it had been a mistake. The beast caught the rock with both hands and hurled it straight back at him. Seth quickly elevated himself even higher to dodge the projectile, the massive boulder bouncing harmlessly off the giant earthen tower. He created another giant rock, and as it fell another one appeared in its place, and then another, and more and more, each one a bit bigger than the last. He saw from his high perch that while the creature caught the first rock, the second made it wobble a little, and the third caused it to fall. The rest of the rocks fell square on top of the thing and spread its metallic fluid across the ground.

Seth slowly lowered himself to the ground via his dirt column, to inspect the debris. This time he was inspecting it while keeping himself ready for another sudden flailing-arm attack. One of the rocks flew at Seth, almost knocking his head off as he ducked. He turned to see the creature standing there once more, with a huge boulder held high above its head. Seth fired an extremely fast blast of air at the beast and temporarily cut it in half, causing it to drop the azurite boulder. But its gooey body sewed itself back together as quick as it had been disassembled. He fired more blades of air at the beast, but it just kept repairing itself.

Seth was starting to get fed up; how can something so simple-minded, something clearly operating only on instinct, be so cunning? Where did it come from? Seth clearly had to think up a new strategy if he was to defeat it. But he needed *time* to think. He erected four azurite walls around the beast, each wall made of stone three metres thick. He could still hear the creature thumping angrily, but he had at least bought himself some time.

Thump. Thump. Thump. Thump. Thump.

Seth turned to the rock.

"Shut up! I'm trying to think!" and he drew the four walls closer together to stop it from moving around so much.

Seth the noticed the goo squirt from the opening at the top of the four walls as its prison became too small.

This creature seems to be made of liquid, so any blow from something solid won't do anything, but I seem to be able to reshape it. What if I could shape it into something harmless, he asked himself. On top of the four walls where it had volcanoed out of its temporary prison, Seth saw the liquid gathering to begin forming a new creature. He summoned a huge glass globe around the beast. The globe quickly contracted around the thing. As it started to run out of room inside the ball, it started to take the same form as the globe itself. Seth shrank the globe until there was just the tiniest bubble of air inside; the rest was now metallic goo. The bubble of air disappeared and reappeared at the same frequency as the creature's earlier thumping, but now just made a ticking noise. Seth made the globe a little bit smaller until not even the bubble of air could be seen, nor the tick heard.

Finally, Seth thought, and turned to give a thumbs up to Red, but Seth had no idea where the Restyard was anymore. He spun in a circle, his thumb held up proudly, knowing Red would see it somehow. He looked at the silver globe that was once a formidable opponent, and extracted a tiny sample of the goo by opening a hole in the glass for a fraction of a second. He encompassed the small sample in another small globe, put it in his pocket, and headed towards his fallen segment now resting in the dirt.

As the underside of each segment of Swevender was pointed, the surface on which Seth's small cottage resided was now at a 45-degree angle. He was sure the inside of his house was a mess — well, more of a mess than before. The small pools of algae-filled water had all drained away and a lot of dirt had tumbled over the edge of his segment. Seth groaned at the idea of cleaning all of this up. However, he didn't want to start using his new matter manipulation abilities for gardening; this would defeat the *purpose* of gardening. The inside of his house was a different matter. *That* was finally going to be clean, now that it would be so easy.

Seth climbed up onto his small piece of Swevender. He thought about casting the three spells from Io, Kern and Marsa to begin flying up into the clouds again. Seth felt more at home somewhere up high, even after his year on the Restyard's solid ground. He always liked climbing the three trees of his small 'forest' when he was younger, and floating up high in the clouds just felt right. But Seth didn't know the spells well enough. But maybe he had learned enough to figure out a different solution — he just needed to do so before another gooey monster showed up.

He would need a material in abundance, easily acquired and able to keep his segment afloat. Seth took a deep breath and from the corner of his eye noticed the slight movement of his blonde whiskers. He knew his answer immediately. Air was always available, and used correctly it could keep his segment afloat no problem. One of the things Seth had seen through the bubble Red had identified as a 'tornado', and said it was extremely powerful. The world they had been on when he saw the tornado was one of the most colourful he had ever seen. Nothing lived there, but the one second that Seth had to witness the world revealed its multicoloured sky with pink lightning everywhere. The sky was thick with clouds, constantly swirling with the complex airflow. Slithering from the clouds in several areas were towers of wind, spinning at unthinkable speeds.

In his mind, Seth pictured his segment floating atop an enormous, writhing grey snake of wind, reaching into the clouds. He raised both his hands and the segment started to lift from the ground. Slowly Seth was getting closer and closer to the clouds above. He was going to blow everyone's mind back home — to the citizens of Swevender, outside the Restyard's magic sphere, the descent of their city had happened only ten minutes ago.

Seth's segment tilted forwards, then backwards, then left; Seth had lost control. He slowly lowered the segment again and it started to stabilise. He realised he would need some practice before he could summon a tornado strong enough to get back up to Swevender's altitude. At least he was out of harm's way, so he didn't have to be worried about long, bony-armed monsters attacking him anymore.

There were many clouds in the sky now. Seth looked up and tried to guess which one was Swevender, but there was no clue which it was. The clouds were all moving quite fast so it was possible Seth could no longer even see the cloud cradling the central segment of his home. He was a upset about it, but had had a year to deal with the loss of his home already. And he still had his part of Swevender, broken but not lost. Eventually he will be able to raise himself to the same height as the city. He wondered if there was anyone else who wasn't on the central segment when it all began to fall. Seth kept his eyes peeled as he cruised along on his small tornado, happy with himself for thinking of a way to take his small piece of home on his new adventure.

***

Seth spent the next few weeks floating a hundred metres from the ground on his little piece of Swevender, exploring the barren landscape. When Seth was in the Restyard, Red had spoken of a great shockwave that was responsible for destroying the whole planet, and Swevender along with it. Being so far above the main force of the shockwave protected Swevender from complete obliteration, but it was certainly the reason the cohesion of the city failed. The shockwave most likely came from the one or both of the two element binders — either in an experiment or a fight, according to Red. He had seen the sky open up as massive chunks of moon and mountain rained down, flattening the landscape. He tried his best to observe the whole calamity from where the shockwave originated. At one point he saw something like a giant propellor remove the top of a mountain, but the rest of the interaction was either hidden beyond the horizon or reduced to indistinguishable dots zipping back and forth like duelling mosquitoes.

The two element binders did not get along very well for a long time now, Red said. His master was Iselle. She had a very volatile temperament but was a brilliant element binder. It seemed likely to him that she had once been known as Marsa, one of the conjurers responsible for creating Swevender. The other only element binder that Red had known of was a male called Cobus. He was also a brilliant mind but Red was never so close to him to witness how he applied it. Red never remembered any third element binder being present.

Anything left alive on the surface of the planet was most likely created by the two element binders, otherwise it would not be sturdy enough to survive the shockwave. The creature Seth had encountered was most likely one such creation, explaining its survival and bizarrely durable fluid nature.

The small glass bauble containing the creature's gooey essence started making a small tapping noise. Seth looked at it and noticed that it was now half full, whereas before the small bead had been pure silver. At Swevender University, Seth learned about the expansion and contraction of materials due to temperature. As something got colder it would shrink, sometimes significantly, or sometimes barely unnoticeably, depending on the material's properties. The opposite was true for materials being warmed up; lead, he remembered, had some of the most significant expansion and contraction rates known, and was a material rarely found on Swevender. Water was the one exception to this rule. As it got colder it the vapour condensed into a fluid, but grew bigger again as the liquid further transformed into ice. This unique reaction to temperature gave the residents of Swevender extra reverence for their most holy element.

FALLEN WORLD

Seth looked at the ticking silvery bead and realised the creature back on the planet's surface would most likely escape if it also contracted at his sample's rate. Any drop in temperature could provide the gooey creature with enough room to swing its giant arms and smash its way out of its crystal prison. Seth reminded himself that he was safe and sound, up high on his small concrete platform, and needn't worry anymore.

The garden on his segment was now back to normal, but the water was now crystal clear. Seth had managed to save a lot of his vegetable garden, making sure he had something to eat. Seth allowed an exception for the use of his abilities when it came to fruits and vegetables. He used them freely to create some of the tastiest crops he had ever grown. The inside of his house was also much cleaner now, but there was still one corner where all the mess had been pushed; Seth didn't want to throw anything away for fear that it would contain a material he could use to his advantage someday. Rather than actively searching the pile for useful samples during his free time, he preferred to avoid the situation. His new abilities made it extremely easy to create — like a whole extra floor on his house, giving Seth more room to create a new mess.

In the beginning Seth felt almost omnipotent thanks to his new found abilities, but his fight with the liquid metal beast quickly made him realise there was much more to learn. Now Seth was mostly just feeling lonely. He hadn't seen anybody for weeks now, nor any movement on the world beneath him since his descent from Swevender. So Seth tried to occupy himself by honing his abilities. During the day he would sail his ship across the landscape atop a mini tornado — hopefully in the right direction. He used the sun as his guide. During the night he would dock his concrete ship on a smooth, towering column of concrete almost two kilometres high. Seth found it hard to breathe at this altitude and had to create a small bubble around his home for the night to provide himself with enough oxygen.

There was clearly more to raising his small ship up to its original altitude than he initially thought.

It was getting dark now, so Seth decided to park his ship on its concrete tower for the night. He decided to test out the sample of the creature before getting some sleep. He had neatly placed the small bead containing the creature's essence into a ring of silver. He held up his hand and focused on using this essence as a source of energy. He began sweating a little from the intensity of his concentration. Suddenly the world around Seth seemed to be getting further and further away. Within seconds he was a few centimetres from the ground, then his surroundings turned dark, and he felt himself falling, tumbling in nothingness.

"Why does this keep happening to me?" shouted Seth as he fell into oblivion.

FALLEN WORLD

Chapter 4

Giant blue spheres filled the surrounding darkness. There were hundreds, as far as the eye could see. The texture of each sphere was so smooth they looked unreal. The light was so low that the huge globes almost looked like flat circles, only defined by their movement upwards. Between some of the orbs, lightning could be seen snaking around as if it was struggling to break free from confinement. Everything was getting closer and increasing in size — smaller creatures became visible on the surfaces of the great globes. Each one was a bipedal creature, with two arms and two legs, but also made up of globes of varying colours. Some orbs were extremely rich in colour with sapphire and ruby reds dancing across their surfaces, while others were a plain grey with delicate imperfections.

The orbs actually resembled planets, something Seth had learned about inside the Restyard that had intrigued him greatly. According to Red, people lived on planets — in fact, Seth lived on a city floating *above* a planet. Seth had found it hard to understand a planet's spherical nature, since his short experience *on* the planet gave the impression it was flat. For him, the general rule was "what goes up, must come down". Surely if everyone lived on a ball, then half of them would be hanging on for dear life at all times... But Seth learned that planets were absolutely humongous, beyond his comprehension — but these creatures were *made* from them! These ones looked almost as tall as Seth.

Each creature was made from ten planets. The central sphere of each was at least double the size of its adjacent planets and resembled a sun. The legs of the being were each made from two planets, sticking out from the bottom of the central globe. The two arms were also made from two planetoids, but they were sticking out from the side of the central globe. One last sphere on top gave the idea of a head on a big round body. These strange beings were slowly moving along the surface of each tremendous blue orb, without walking or really moving their bodies at all, just slowly gliding along in a petite, choreographed ballet.

Seth had been so engrossed in observing his surreal environment, he realised he hadn't taken a breath for quite some time. He found his attempt to breathe in to be ineffective. Seth tried again, but still nothing. There did seem to be a lack of wind despite Seth continuing to plunge, so he surmised there was no air in this place — wherever he was. He would need to make an air bubble like the one he used to sleep at altitude. Seth looked around vainly for oxygen.

He didn't know how much air was left in his lungs, so he knew he had to solve this problem soon. But not much air left in his lungs meant there was still *some*. Seth took a risk and breathed out what could be his last breath. He held his hand in front of his mouth to give him some perception of the breath, then manifested more air in his immediate vicinity.

Seth tried breathing in and found it wasn't quite the right proportion of oxygen; he was able to breathe again but each breath was getting increasingly difficult. Beneath him a colossal blue surface was coming towards him, now at an accelerated rate. Seth used his ring with a water-filled bead as the catalyst for creating a small propeller beneath, slowing his descent. It was hard to tell how close the smooth surface was — except for the small being on the surface now growing larger. Seth felt like he was finally falling at a safe speed when he hit the ground suddenly, knocking precious air out of his lungs.

Seth stood up and saw the strange being, made of planets, skating across the surface towards him. He wasn't sure what had just happened. It seemed like the sample of the gooey monster had teleported him to another universe. Nothing looked familiar here and the lack of oxygen made it seem like nothing alive was supposed to be here either, unless it was one of these strange planet people. Most of the beings gliding along the surrounding blue surface had an incredibly bright central section and could be seen from very far away. Seth reached out to the one approaching him now and felt intense warmth coming from the bright burning centre of the being. He decided against touching it due to the fact that it resembled a small sun, which didn't have a reputation for rewarding people for physical contact.

"Hello, I'm sorry, but where exactly are we?" Seth asked the approaching being, it froze suddenly a few metres away from him and slowly turned towards him, but said nothing. Seth attempted some more verbal interactions with the ball being, but it remained silent as it became stationary. Seth sighed and thought he would have to teleport again. Then hopefully he could get a bearing on where he was… He looked at the ring on his finger containing the metallic ooze and concentrated on the small bead once more. Behind the bead, he noticed that one of the globes of the catatonic ball being was different from the rest: it had brilliant blues and greens scattered across its surface. Above those small islands of colour, white spiralling smoke spread in a flat layer just above the main surface of the globe and cast a small shadow onto its surface. A stripe in the middle of the planet was the most colourful area, while the side closest to the 'sun' of the being's central sphere was bathed in bright light. The opposite side was almost pitch black. Seth looked back at the silver bead on his finger, returned to concentrating and once again his surroundings suddenly changed.

He was falling again, this time towards a scene that looked more familiar to him. The ground was covered in long, green grass, and tall twisted trees sporadically sprouted up across its surface. Seth gasped, and found his breathing felt normal now; apparently, he had teleported to a much less hostile environment. It reminded him a bit of Swevender, with its emerald grass and the occasional tree. With ample air around him, Seth was able to manipulate the air flow to lower himself steadily to the ground. He noticed he was having some difficulty with the manipulation and hit the ground just a little too fast, leaving him short of breath.

He took in his surroundings: all the trees around him had a dark, almost black bark covering their trunks. Only a few small branches were sticking out below the fifty metre level, while higher up the tree's growth thickened significantly, blocking any sun from reaching the ground directly below. Each tree had a bare dirt surface around its base with only a few small green sprouts poking up. However, the grass beyond the trees' shadows was extremely thick and would prove difficult to navigate. Seth breathed in deeply through his nose, then summoned his water scope and held it up to inspect the distant surroundings. He saw an extremely odd structure jutting out of the ground higher than any of the trees around it, its form clearly not natural and therefore indicating some kind of civilisation. The structure was a few kilometres away. Seth started walking in its direction, hoping it wasn't populated by non-responsive planetoid beings.

Halfway to the building-shaped object, Seth had begun travelling via sharp bursts of air allowing him to make huge leaps through the air when the grass became irritating to walk through. Plus, he was sure he had seen some strange creatures slipping between the blades of grass earlier... As he travelled, he noticed again that his powers felt weaker, or something was hindering them, making flying rather difficult. The faster he went, the less control Seth had over the surrounding air. Seth lost control and tumbled a few times. He attempted to lift himself with air again after a small stumble, but now there was not even enough power to lift him. Seth was puzzled. He tried creating a propeller of water using his ring, which seemed to work fine, so Seth continued forward in this manner. He did reflect on how he should try not to let his abilities make him lazy, but in this case it was a matter of safety and time, he justified.

Eventually the structure was within what Seth thought to be a walkable distance, so he jumped to the ground and continued by foot. In the absence of the wind whistling in his ears, Seth started to hear a strange tone every now and then. **Ding**. He didn't know what it was but it was occurring at regular intervals and was the same tone each time. It did not seem to get louder as he approached what he thought was the source, instead always remaining somewhere off in the distance. **Ding**.

Seth arrived at the base of the structure. It was huge and rectangular, reaching up about 150 metres. Next to this building was another one about fifty metres taller. Both of them had intricate metal pipes infesting every inch of their surface. Some pipes were much newer than others, while some had been corroded through. It looked like the building had been repaired a hundred times, but each time the old part was never discarded or replaced. Beneath a complicated lattice of conduits at the base of the smaller building was what appeared to be a door. Seth walked up to it and raised his hand to knock. *Knock knock.* He tried a few times but got no response. The other building did not even have a door — or if it did, it was now lost to a web of pipelines.

Seth looked around and noticed there was an entire village nearby these two buildings. He could see many humble houses made of wood, most with a material that seemed like curved, orange concrete tiles, laid out in a grid pattern forming a point. Some of the houses had walls made of red stone bricks. Sticking out occasionally between the buildings were thin poles, all with the same strange contraption at the top: three cones pointing inwards with their apexes touching, with their larger bases gaping open and angled outwards. The three cones had a smaller cylinder visible inside them making them look like three daffodils standing back-to-back, without petals.

As Seth walked towards the village he heard that strange tone again. **Ding**. He then saw people walking around the village — it seemed to be a normal enough place, unlike the first two buildings he had encountered. It was a lot smaller than Swevender and fewer trees. The inhabitants shuffled around slowly and seemed to be paying him very little attention. Some did stop very briefly to acknowledge Seth and would mumble something incoherent. Seth thought he could hear Common, but then they would use a word that sounded like nothing he had ever heard before.

One of the people approached Seth. He was wearing a grey uniform with a belt holstering what looked like effective tools for bludgeoning someone. He held up his hand in a manner that indicated Seth should stop.

"Who are you?" asked the man in a deep, bellowing voice.

His uniform looked quite sharp, with a few black stripes intended to emphasise the bulk of his shoulders — they now emphasised the curve of his protrusive belly. His face was occupied by a formidable dark brown moustache and hair of the same colour poked out from underneath his small, rimless hat.

Seth was relieved it was actually Common that he had heard.

"My name is Seth Cost" he replied. "Where is this?"

The man was holding one of his bludgeoning instruments, pointed it at Seth and said from behind a thick moustache,

"I'll be asking the raggles here, young man!"

Uh oh, thought Seth to himself.

"Uhhh, what?" he replied, puzzled by the unfamiliar word.

"Where did you come from and what are you mirring here?" asked the man.

All Seth could see was a moustache moving around, completely covering the man's mouth. *I guess it's a different kind of Common.* Seth noted that in the context he could probably understand it.

"What I am mirring sir, is looking for someone who can tell me where I am," Seth replied, holding both his hands up in a sort of defensive manner. The moustached man raised one eyebrow and looked Seth up and down, inspecting his strange fashion.

"You jink tarin and you talk funny, boy."

Seth assumed 'jink tarin' was in reference to his clothes, and found himself adjusting his robes self-consciously.

"This is Chos Garren Village, and you better be on your best tractum while you're here, boy," said the man as he put his cudgel back in his belt. The cudgel had two small dots near the base where the man was holding it.

"I suggest you go about your business peacefully," he said to Seth.

"No problem. I am not here to cause any problems, just wanted to find out where I am so I can go back home," Seth replied calmly.

Mr. Moustache pointed to Seth's left.

"You can buy yourself a verhil in the market stildrum."

He looked as puzzled as Seth felt; this language seemed to only have occasional differences, but it was always something miles away from the word he expected to hear. He didn't know for sure what a verhil was, but as it would apparently help him find out where he was, he headed for the market stildrum.

Seth approached what he assumed was a market stand. They seemed to be selling food — all sorts of vegetables he had never seen before. One looked like a zucchini with orange peel for skin, with a small flower sticking from the top of each one. There was also a small green apple, but poking from its skin were small spikes tapering off into tiny coils. Seth looked up at the shopkeeper who had been watching him, waiting patiently to hear any questions.

"Hi" Seth said in a friendly tone. "Would you happen to have a… uh verhil for me?"

The man laughed a little.

"No, sorry boy, this is a pilm shop. You can find a verhil three stalls up." He gestured a little further up the dirt road. Seth was getting a little tired of being called "boy" and "young man" everywhere he went. He had hoped his goatee would have stopped this condescending nickname.

Ding.

Seth heard the strange tone again. He stopped to listen in case it happened again, then said "thank you" to the shopkeeper. He saw the puzzled look in the man's face just as he turned to leave for the other store, but ignored it.

Seth arrived at the stall the previous shopkeeper had indicated. There was no one attending the shop now. Seth looked at the objects on display. The little building had three levels; the owner must have sold verhils downstairs and lived on the upper floor. The whole house was made from a dark wood that looked to be very sturdy. He thought he might be able to use it for his own material manipulation experiments, and began picking at a wooden pillar that was holding up a section of the building. A small piece came off and landed in his waiting hand just as the shop owner came out. She was an attractive woman, probably in her early thirties with long and wavy fiery-orange coloured hair. She had numerous freckles across her cheeks, and glasses with a thick black rim emphasised the size and hue of her bright blue eyes. She was about one head shorter than Seth and had her hands on her hips.

"What the spizz are you mirring to my home?" she snapped.

Seth looked guiltily at her while she glared angrily.

"My apologies! I have a nervous habit where I begin picking at things when kept waiting," he responded in a friendly tone, hoping to reduce the tension in the air — although subtly complaining didn't really help. *She should have been attending her shop though*, Seth thought.

"Hrmph. I saw you shaverse here — you barely waited two seconds before you attempted to tear my house down!" She said aggressively. She blew away one of her orange curls of hair that had fallen across her face. Seth let the piece of wood fall to the ground.

"I am truly sorry ma'am. I don't believe that speck of wood will contribute to the eventual collapse of your house though... I was just coming here to acquire a verhil from you." Seth hoped he was pronouncing it correctly.

"No grollarin young man, just mir not pick my house to pieces. Mir you want a verhil of just Chos Garren or the village including the surrounding norotory?"

Seth needed more than just a map of the village to find his way back home, so he replied,

"Ummm, the second thing you said."

She handed him a verhil. Seth looked at the folded piece of paper: 'verhil' meant 'map'. Seth was sure that a map wasn't going to help his situation much. He had no idea what he would need to look for on a map, and the landscape from which he had come from was completely decimated; he had no reference points.

The orange haired woman held out her hand.

"That will be seven grilliks, young man."

Seth quickly unfolded the map to inspect it and, as he suspected, it revealed nothing to him. Seth realised getting back to his own world was going to be more difficult than he initially envisioned. The woman asking him for money was now becoming a little impatient. He smiled a bit awkwardly and handed the map back to her.

"Sorry, but this is not what I was looking for."

"I'm sorry. I thought you wanted a verhil. This is the best Chos Garren has to offer boy!" The orange haired woman snatched the map back hastily.

"To be honest I come from very far away — too far away. What I need is a map showing me how to get back to the blue sphere place. And my name is not 'boy', it is Seth." Seth tried not to sound too desperate as he explained his situation.

The woman raised one eyebrow and looked at Seth over her glasses.

"Well then, now I can tell people there is a boy named Seth walking around Chos Garren speaking nonsense, instead of just a nameless boy wearing a blue dress."

"It's not a dress, it's a robe. This outfit is quite appropriate for a wa— matter manipulator, ma'am. And I am *not* speaking nonsense; not one hour ago, I was looking at a creature made of planets, surrounded by enormous turquoise-coloured orbs. Where is that place from here?" Seth asked rather defensively. He wasn't sure if he was giving away too much information, but he assumed honesty would be the best way to find the path back home.

"Well I am not called 'ma'am', Seth, my name is Katja. And I think your chip is affecting your brain. I've not heard so much nonsense in my whole life! Turquoise orbs? Creatures made of planets? If you mir not want a verhil, please make way for other clunders who actually want to buy something." Katja waved her hand in a dismissive gesture.

As Seth moved aside for someone else who wanted the assorted paper-related items Katja had to offer, he realised maybe a map would help in the end anyway.

"Sorry to bother you again Katja, but I think I would like to buy a verhil from you after all. How much is the verhil showing only this lovely town you live in?" Seth did his best to act friendly; he had an inkling that Katja had a right to be annoyed with him now. Katja rolled her eyes and placed her hands on her hips again. She sighed somewhat pointedly and handed a map to Seth.

"Five grilliks."

Seth was about to confess that he had no grilliks to speak of, knowing it would probably irritate Katja even further and she would send him on his way. Then the other customer handed Katja some small brass coins, which she reciprocated with a folded-up piece of paper covered in many parallel blue lines and countless small blue dots.

In the process of the transaction, the customer dropped a coin, which rolled from the table and landed at Seth's feet. He smiled at his luck and picked it up, studying it quickly, and attempted to use his matter manipulation techniques to replicate more of them inside his pocket. But once again, it seemed Seth's powers were failing him; his pocket should have begun sagging within seconds from the weight of all the grilliks appearing inside it. There must be something about this world's matter that was incompatible with Seth's power. He could summon his water propeller with no problem, but flying with air here didn't seem to work at all anymore — and now this coin was messing up Seth's plans too. Seth was still staring at the coin when he noticed Katja and the customer were both looking at him. He quickly handed the coin back to the customer, hoping he had done it quick enough not to arouse any suspicion that he was contemplating its theft. Seth needed one of those coins. Then he could use one of his own rings of a similar metal to create some duplicates.

Seth looked at Katja still waiting for him to hand her five grilliks.

"Actually, I would like to sell *you* something." Seth took off his gold ring (he still hadn't found a purpose for it), and secretly replicated another one in his pocket.

"This ring is made of pure gold, and I want only one grillik for it."

Katja's eyes opened wide. She grabbed the ring and looked at it skeptically. She held it flat in her palm as if to test the weight, and she put it on each of her fingers to find a good fit.

She breathed in sharply.

"Well, I mir not know what 'gold' is, but the ring looks prillisly well-made and it has a nice colour, like the colour of grilliks, so one grillik is a fair price."

Seth smiled as he held his hand out to receive his grillik for the gold ring. His other hand was in his pocket, fiddling with the new gold ring he had just made. Seth put it on unconsciously and then held up the coin to study it. He flipped it around in between his index finger and thumb to get a good gauge of its dimensions and intricate carvings. *Katja was right*, Seth thought. His ring was indeed the same colour as the coin. He used his gold ring to create a handful of grilliks in his pocket. Seth's robe drooped to one side as the gold coins pulled on it. Seth pulled what felt like five coins from his pocket to hand over to Katja. Katja gracefully handed the map to Seth and placed the grilliks into her own pocket. She adjusted her glasses a little as her eyes followed the hand wearing the new gold ring and spoke to Seth in a somewhat exaggerated tone.

"Kesson."

Before Seth could thank her, she turned away to return to her hidden vantage point above her stall.

A jingling noise came from Seth's pocket while he walked. He pulled out his map and tried to become acquainted with the small village of Chos Garren. He could see the small dirt road used to lead people through the marketplace — where he was — and to the east (if Seth was reading the map correctly) lay a series of buildings placed in no particular order or pattern, but they seemed to have roughly similar distances between them. To the west of the marketplace were more houses, most likely residential and, due to their dramatic increase in size, clearly owned by the wealthier residents of Chos Garren. Another dirt road snaked through the village and broke off into smaller paths leading to each house. One broad path led to the north of the marketplace, where there were no houses, only structures of a sort Seth could not recognise.

The map showed the two pipe buildings also, but there was no road leading to them. Seth had expected the largest road of all to lead there. They seemed quite significant, given that they were gigantic in comparison to every other building in Chos Garren, and made of a completely different material.

Ding.

There were also some blue circles dotting the drawing occasionally — Seth was almost standing on top of one, according to the map. He looked around and saw a pole topped with the same triple-coned device from earlier.

Seth needed to find someone who could answer his questions. His last conversation had just raised more: what did Katja mean when she said, "I think your chip is affecting your brain"? He didn't know what a chip was nor why she assumed he had one in his brain. He looked up from the map and saw a tall man shuffling slowly along in front of him. Seth raised his hand and opened his mouth to ask a question, but the man turned to Seth with tears running down his cheeks. The sadness on the man's face made Seth want to cry in turn and he felt water begin to accumulate in the corners of his eyes. The man looked like he had been crying for years; his shirt had a darker patch around the neck from where the tears had stained it. Seth decided he would do better to find someone a little less depressing to ask for help, and lowered his hand. The tall man shrugged his shoulders and continued to shuffle along, leaving trails in the dirt behind him.

There seemed to be a lot of people in the same situation as the tall man, tears running down their cheeks constantly. Seth almost began to wish he was back in the strange blue land of the planet people; at least they weren't so bloody depressing. Someone important must have died, and they must have been very loved. But then Seth passed people with smiles on their faces so wide, their skulls threatened to pop out of their heads.

Seth tried asking one of the deliriously happy residents for information, a rounder blonde lady about forty years old.

"Excuse me, but do you know this area?"

It seemed a fairly reasonable question to Seth, but the lady's reaction indicated otherwise. She began spinning around on the spot, then jumped up and down four times, shouting "Yes I mir!" as she ran away from him, her grin still stretching from ear to ear. Chos Garren was getting weirder by the minute.

Chapter 5

Chos Garren was a very strange town indeed. The houses all seemed to be made of the same materials: wood and something that Seth discovered was called clay. It was apparently readily found by digging into the soil or in exposed riverbeds. The clay would be dug up and then left outside during the winter to freeze. The frozen clay would then be broken up and thawed out; the process would then be repeated several times. The freezing and unfreezing allowed for higher quality clay to be made, and when it was mixed with the correct ratio of water, it would become a malleable substance. This allowed the people of Chos Garren to create tiles and bricks for their homes. Seth had never seen any clay in Swevender so he was very fascinated by it and made sure to find a sample to bring with him (although it had proved to be unaffected by Seth's powers here).

The citizens seemed to go about their business as normal and the **ding** that Seth still could not pinpoint continued to occur at regular intervals. The citizens of Chos Garren seemed to be a very emotional lot; very rarely was someone walking by without some kind of strong feeling shining from their face. Some were sad to the point of crying, while others smiled so widely they looked slightly deranged. Seth had to hear the explanation about clay from a man in between sobs: he bawled the whole mining process to Seth.

While exploring, Seth had gotten a little hungry. He went back to the pilm shop to try some of the strange food there. He got some odd looks from the owner of the shop while Seth asked him what everything was and what each thing tasted like. The orange skin zucchini he had seen earlier was called a 'reen' and you could also eat the flower sticking out of it — Seth discovered a little too late that that was an extremely spicy experience. He tried some round berries with a bright purple skin, and found their sweetness helped dull the burning from the reen flower. These berries were called 'russocks'. A thin brown stick with a strange apple-shaped fruit had piqued Seth's curiosity. The fruit on the end of the stick was covered in tiny red berries, each with a small black seed in its centre. The seeds and the stick were also edible; this fruit was called a 'chusst'. Its natural handle made it a practical sort of food to take with him on the rest of his exploration of the village.

The map that Seth had bought earlier only helped him become familiar with the village; it hadn't helped provide any clue as to where he was and how he could make his way back home. He was starting to think he might be stuck here. Almost every person that Seth had asked for help had given crazy answers and seemed completely demented. When he did find someone even slightly normal, his elation was so great he ended up giving them the impression that *he* was also one of the hysterical weirdos walking around. Seth was starting to get a bit annoyed — especially with the happy people. What in Io's name were they all so damn cheery about?

The most normal conversation Seth had had in this strange town was with Katja. Even though they hadn't parted on the best terms, he decided she could supply the most information, with minimal questioning. She hadn't shown any signs of being unnaturally happy or sad… she did seem a bit angry, but that was mostly his own fault, Seth reflected as he thought back on his conversation with her. He picked out the marketplace on his map and started back towards her stall.

Once again, there was no one attending the shop. Seth decided to try waiting patiently this time; no sense in irritating Katja even further. No one appeared for a minute, but Seth was sure she could see him from wherever she was and just didn't feel like serving him. He was momentarily tempted to start picking at the same piece of wood from earlier, but he quickly decided against that if he wanted Katja to be cooperative. He knocked on the table and waited. Then he shouted hello. Ten seconds later, Katja finally appeared, coming out of a door behind her display of various paper goods. She assumed her favourite stance: hands on hips and a disapproving look.

"You're back. Did you have trouble reading your verhil?" asked Katja in a slightly sarcastic tone, but with a smile in her voice. Apparently she was not *so* irritated with Seth.

He pulled the map from his pocket and gestured towards it.

"No no, this is hands down the best verhil I have ever owned, nothing wrong with it!"

Katja laughed gently as she folded her arms.

"Spare me the himmus, boy. What mir you want?"

Ding.

Seth was slightly distracted as he heard that noise again. Recently it had blended into the ambient noise and Seth hadn't even noticed it during his previous hour of exploration. He wasn't sure what question to ask first, but he tried:

"Who around here knows where I came from?" He knew how stupid the question sounded before he finished it.

"Ha! Well I would hope that would be you, Seth. You are really a tarin guy! You would get along with my man; he is also a bit of a philosopher," chuckled Katja.

Seth took a deep breath before his next question, hoping he could assemble some sort of logic:

"What's with all the crying people in this town? I swear about half the people I see are sad about something." Katja's eyebrow lifted as she gave Seth a confused look.

"That is called community service — but how can you not know that? Anyone with a chip knows what that is, and the only people without chips are the Inquirers. You an Inquirer, boy?"

"Well that just raises more uh, raggles! How is crying community service?" he asked, a little frustrated. Seth's question

FALLEN WORLD

had just confused matters even further for him. Katja smiled, showing she was clearly amused at Seth's confusion.

"You really are not from around here. I will tell you what you want to know, young Seth, but it's going to teth you. From that jingling coming your dress pocket, it seems like you can afford it." She gestured to the pocket sagging under the weight of the grilliks he had replicated earlier.

Seth put his hand into his pocket and held up one of the grilliks between his finger and thumb. He closed one eye while he looked at it.

"You are right, I don't know where I am from, and it's definitely not here."

Next to the coin in Seth's hand materialised an exact copy, falling to the stall's countertop. It was immediately replaced by another one, then another and another until the small stall had grilliks scattered all over its surface. Katjas eyes had widened in disbelief, looking around at the coins in front of her.

"H-how? That is amazing! ... And how?" was Katja's reply to Seth's display. Seth smiled a little, happy his small coin trick had turned the tables on the nonsense-talking.

"It's a simple matter of becoming acquainted with the form and shape, and then the particles making up the matter. I was spared the need to imagine the object since I had one in my hand." Seth knew this answer would not satisfy Katja and could hopefully turn the tables in his favour.

"Can I ask you some more raggles then?" Seth asked.

Katja started to collect the grilliks lying on her table.

"You can ask whatever you want if you pay so generously Seth. I won't need to sell any more verhils today! Come inside and you can ask all the raggles you like." Seth followed Katja upstairs into her house.

The interior of Katja's house was rather cosy. Being the owner of a shop that sold a multitude of paper products, she had decorated the walls with many different images. A lot of them looked like maps, while some seemed to be people in dramatic poses. There was also a painting of a large flower, resembling the reen flower that Seth had eaten earlier. A few rugs were placed at overlapping intervals, covering most of the wooden floor. The rugs had complex patterns made of reds, oranges, yellows and blues. There was a bookcase, barely half full, on the wall opposite the stairs where the two had entered. Behind the bookcase was another staircase leading to a higher floor, but they ascended no further. In front of them were a few wooden chairs surrounding a small table where Katja had indicated they would be holding their conversation.

By the end of the conversation Seth felt like he was a step closer to finding his way home. He now knew how different this place was from his home; not just Chos Garren, but the land in which it resided, too. First of all, the citizens of Chos Garren had chips in their heads. The chips were responsible for controlling people's emotions with something called 'clase'. Clase would determine if someone would feel predominantly happy, sad, angry or so on. People were rewarded for good behaviour by being given a boost in their mood, making them happy. Anyone who broke a law could be instantly and painfully disabled when their clase was activated, and would serve a sentence of "community service" being driven to tears by clase; the length of the term depended on the severity of their crime. There was a similar system in Swevender, it was just that clase had nothing to do with it.

Katja herself wasn't deliriously happy or sad. She had recently finished serving a short sentence of community service and her clase was now set to neutral, she told Seth. She also explained how this was the one moment where citizens had a little clarity. The mustachioed man Seth had encountered when he first arrived in Chos Garren was part of town security. His clase kept him alert and a little hostile. He was the same man that had caught Katja committing her crime (Katja seemed very reluctant to admit what the actual crime was).The clase was not something of which she spoke fondly, nor community service; it seemed a traumatic thing to be forced to cry for months at a time. Some people had committed crimes so heinous that their clase was permanently set to melancholy and they would never be able to be happy again.

The Inquirers were the ones who initiated this method of keeping the peace. According to Katja the Inquirers were not nice people, but they were to be feared. They controlled Chos Garren. The Inquirers lived inside the two pipe-covered buildings Seth had seen earlier. These were known as the Reference Centre and none of the town's citizens were permitted to enter. Nobody knew what the Inquirers did in there, but they rarely needed to come out so nobody actually knew what they looked like anymore. Any stories about them depicted the Inquirers as older gentleman, wearing white trench coats on top of the finest fabrics with devices that performed incredible acts — as incredible as Seth's ability to materialise coins out of nothing.

The world on which Chos Garren resided was also somewhat confusing to Seth. Katja tried her best but was not able to explain fully. Chos Garren was a village on a continent called Grael, located in the central arc of the world Estever. Estever was the name of the planet, which could also be the planet Seth was from for all he knew; after all, he only recently learned he had been on a city floating *above* a planet. But Estever wasn't pure dirt and stone so it seemed likely to be somewhere other than Seth's place of origin. Estever had three major sections, called arcs. Only the central arc was inhabited by humans. The blazing arc was sunwards, an extremely inhospitable environment. The further sunwards anyone walked, the hotter and dryer it became, and the sun became blindingly bright extremely quick. Not many people had travelled very far into the blazing arc as they had no real protection for such extreme heat. The shadow arc was the exact opposite: it was extremely cold, becoming colder the closer one came to 'the absence', which was the area of the shadow arc where absolutely no light could reach. It had a reputation for sending people insane. The shadow arc had been explored a few times by the most ambitious of adventurers and was renowned for strange beasts prowling the barren landscapes. Every creature from the shadow arc tended to come with a very vague description, only ever seen in torchlight or darkness.

Katja also had questions for Seth: she hadn't met anyone who was able to pull money from thin air and wanted to know his secret. Unfortunately, it wasn't really something that could be explained or taught so quickly. Seth summarised his power by saying it came from focus and knowing that everything was made of smaller particles which had power to be exploited. This only seemed to cause more questions. Seth performed a few more examples of his power by providing Katja with a pile of grilliks. He also created a new balcony for her house using one of his rings of grey stone. At 22 years of age, Seth's hormones were definitely causing him to be a little friendlier to Katja than normal; he took pleasure in showing her how little effort it took him to create such things. After a few hours it became apparent that the sky had held a sunset for the last few hours, even though no sun could be seen. Katja explained that this was just how it was in Estever. Their sun did not have cycles like where Seth was from, but was permanently fixed in the same place. Most of the population lived in the small belt of the planet where the sun provided enough light to live normally, but not too much heat. The sun was – according to Katja – partially inside the planet, meaning it was constantly grinding the pole of the blazing arc.

This world made no sense to Seth. He had teleported himself very far away from home indeed. As he spoke of his situation to Katja, she mentioned a resistance group that were rumoured to live in the shadow arc. They had managed to create technology forbidden by the Inquirers, making permanent sources of light allowing them to live in the shadow arc comfortably. Apparently they also used their technology to extract the chips placed in their brains by the Inquirers.

After all this talk Seth started to yawn from lack of sleep. He didn't realise there was no night in Estever, and had been waiting for the sun to set. Katja was more than happy to accommodate him, but explained she would have to check with her man, who walked in just as Katja was explaining the system of Estever's sun.

"Who is this young lad Kat? And did you build a new casner on the house today?" came a hoarse voice from the stairway, accompanied by the thumping of heavy boots on the steps. From the hole in the ground poked the head of Katja's man. His face was covered by black, shaggy hair; only eyes, nose and a little bit of cheek could be seen. The majority of the hair growing from his head had been tied back to make him look a little less like a sea urchin on a human body, a body with a proudly bulging belly.

The man stood, waiting for an answer. Katja rose to give him a 'welcome home' hug.

"Boris, this is Seth — umm... Cost. He is from very far away, and he is responsible for the casner and the pile of grilliks." She gestured towards the table where a sizeable pile of money lay. Boris' eyes widened, looking first at Seth, then at the table and at the door leading to their new balcony. It looked like he smiled after he had worked out the situation, but it was hard to tell with so much of his face being hidden behind wiry black hair. Boris was a little shorter than Seth. He was wearing a grey, collarless shirt, with a dark brown leather vest and grey canvas pants.

"It's a pleasure to meet you, young man, but for what stalusion would we be giving you so many grilliks? Surely a casner is not so dear?" asked Boris while placing his bag down on the floor. Katja put her hand on Boris' shoulder and whispered an explanation for the grilliks on the table.

"Oh the grilliks are *from* you. Well then, it is an *extra* great pleasure to meet you, Seth." Boris sat down on the chair next to Seth and picked up one of the coins, inspecting it.
Seth smiled.

"Likewise. I have been having a bit of trouble acquainting myself with Chos Garren and Katja was a great help. I still don't know how to get home, but I think I am going to try find that resistance she was mentioning, in the shadow arc."

Boris looked strangely at Katja.

"What resistance might that be young man? I told you that wasn't true Kat, mir not send the poor guy into the shadow arc looking for something that's not even there."
Katja whispered into Boris' ear again, and he shook his head, audibly saying no. They continued to communicate this way for a while, sometimes glancing back at Seth.
Boris eventually turned back to Seth.

"Listen you can stay here tonight, but tomorrow you will have to find yourself somewhere else to rest. And take your grilliks; we are fine without them."
Seth was a little irritated. He expected Boris to be a pragmatic person, like Katja seemed to be, but he needed sleep so he gracefully thanked Boris and Katja for letting him stay. Katja didn't look too happy with Boris's decision but she went with it. She cooked dinner for all three of them, and very little was said throughout the whole cooking and eating process.
Seth enjoyed the meal thoroughly despite the atmosphere. During the awkward silence Seth began to hum a song to himself which gained scrunched-up looks of disapproval from both Katja and Boris. Seth very rarely had the chance to eat meat in Swevender, and even less since he left, so he almost inhaled his steak when it was placed in front of him. Accompanying the

steak was a vegetable the same consistency as a boiled potato, but it was bright yellow and much sweeter. On his plate he also found curved orange rods, both ends wider than the middle. They had a crunchiness similar to apples, but were a little salty. Seth also found a familiar-looking flower which he pushed to the side.

When Boris finished his meal, he picked up everyone's dishes and placed them back by the stove. He walked back downstairs, and Seth could hear some noises outside of wood being banged about. Boris returned upstairs shortly, then looked pointedly at Kat.

"I am going to bed Kat, I'll see you soon."
She nodded her head at him in acknowledgement and moved to where Boris had placed the dishes. She stacked them so she could easily carry them downstairs.

"I am just going to rinse the dishes Seth. You will have to use the floor to sleep, I mir not really have anything else." Katja seemed a little saddened by her man's recent actions as she walked downstairs.

Seth moved his hands in an attempt to levitate the dishes from Katja's hands, but remembered his powers didn't work right on Estever. Katja gave Seth a strange look as he waved his hands around ineffectually. He instinctively tried to correct his mistake and water flew out of his hands, pushing the crockery from Katja's hands. In this process Katja got soaked and one of the plates smashed on the floor; Seth caught the rest.

"What was that for? Now I have to go the market and deal with that terrible Mr. Railson for a new neld!" Katja exclaimed, her whole front dripping with water. Seth's eyes were still wide from the surprise of the smashing plate. He quickly looked at his ring made of steel and a new plate formed from the metal.

"Sorry, I wanted to wash them for you. I will clean that up, and I still insist on washing the rest," said Seth apologetically as he placed the dirty dishes on the table.
From behind Seth came Boris' nasal voice:
"You can throw them all out if you can just trank one out of thin air like that, boy." Boris had come downstairs to see what was amiss when he heard the plate smash. Katja turned to him.
"I told you, this boy has some otherworldly power! He might be useful."
"Not now Katja! Come upstairs and dry yourself off — what were you mirring? And you boy, I will have some raggles for you tomorrow," Boris responded. Katja followed Boris as he walked back upstairs, turning back to Seth just before her head disappeared into the floor above.
"You can cover the innels when you are ready to sleep." she walked upstairs out of view.
Seth assumed she was talking about the windows, and saw a thick roll of material above each one. Each roll had a small ribbon tied around both ends. Seth undid the knots and the blinds unfurled, blocking 100 percent of the light. Seth lay down on a rug next to the table, but could feel straight away he wasn't going to get any sleep on this hard floor. Seth stood up and clicked his fingers. He made a small mattress from the same material as his robe, on which he fell asleep instantly.

FALLEN WORLD

Chapter 6

Ding.

Seth was woken by the noise again. He promised himself he would find out what that was before he left Estever. There was no light entering the room, so he was disoriented at first. Slowly Seth's cognition returned to him and he remembered where he was. He stood up, stretched, and created a small flame for illumination. He opened one of the blinds. Seth was sure Boris wasn't going to be friendly when he came downstairs. He wasn't scared of Boris; the monster he had fought after coming out of the Restyard seemed a much more formidable foe, but Seth did not really feel like going through a whole interrogation. Katja had been nothing but helpful, although it didn't look like she would be divulging any more information as long as Boris was around. The flame in Seth's hand disappeared and he slowly made his way downstairs into the shop. Before leaving, Seth looked behind him one last time and saw the dishes on the table still dirty. He wasn't in the mood for cleaning, so he continued quietly down the stairs.

When Seth was outside again he saw the same familiar sunset sky. He needed to find the resistance Katja spoke about. First he needed to find the shadow arc, which should be extremely easy: just go the opposite direction of the sun. Seth got his bearings, saw where the sun was at its brightest, and started walking in the opposite direction. Being the impatient guy he was, Seth decided to launch into the air on spinning blades of water and started flying towards the shadow arc. A few people saw him and gasped but Seth was past the point of caring — he wasn't sure why he tried to hide his powers in the first place. He looked at the citizens below and could see the structure of the city clearly; the market district, the wealthier district, the gap between the village and the huge pipe towers, and behind the towers, the forest in which he had arrived.

Chos Garren was getting smaller as Seth's propeller levitated him upwards to a nice vantage point. He needed much less water for his propeller nowadays; the year in the Restyard had strengthened his matter manipulation skills. It began to get warmer as he got higher, the opposite of what Seth was used to. He looked around and saw why: the sun was now shining directly on him, no longer hidden beneath the curve of the horizon. He had to protect his eyes from the glare. What Seth saw did not look like a sun, just a great glowing wall in the distance. It was blocked out in some areas by the mountains, but it continued to follow the curvature of the planet. Neither the start nor the end of the sun-wall could be seen, no matter how high Seth got. When he turned around to face the shadow arc again, he was surprised by how suddenly the darkness began. A solid line of shadow was seen in the distance, also following the curve of the planet. Seth was almost at the cloud line now. He slowed his ascent and attempted to get his floating under control. Seth preferred flying via means of manipulating the air around him but the matter from which Estever was made still refused to cooperate.

It took a while but eventually Seth was able to hold himself reasonably still. He began to scan the landscape for any signs of light in the shadow arc. To his surprise, he saw *many* lights, all of them moving around. Some were much brighter than others. None of the lights seemed to indicate some kind of building that might house a resistance. Seth flew towards the shadow arc for closer inspection. He came closer to the ground so he could see what was controlling the moving lights. They didn't seem to be illuminating anything in particular; their purpose must have been to announce a presence. Seth saw a series of multicoloured lights shooting up and down in small stripes, moving so fast he found it hard to count how many individual bands there were. As Seth approached the source, he clicked his fingers and an incredible stream of sparks began flying from his hand to illuminate the area. The source of rainbow coloured lights was something Seth had never seen before: a small translucent dome with hundreds of tiny legs, scurrying around on the ground. The dome was made up of segments, and the line dividing each segment was filled with coloured lights.

The dome started to run away from the light Seth was creating, and he saw that it was dragging two long blue tentacles as it ran, leaving a trail of reflective liquid behind them. Seth, still hovering several metres above the ground, began chasing the strange jelly-like creature (which was rather difficult as it was quite an agile beast with its hundreds of little legs). He was concentrating so hard on the domed creature that his stream of sparks had nearly disappeared. It was easy to understand how people might go insane in the shadow arc: it was *dark*. Seth let the spark shower dwindle to nothing and held his hand up a few centimetres from his face. He saw nothing. He hadn't even travelled very far into the shadow arc and it was already darker than anywhere he had been his entire life. For people who are used to bathing in the light of a permanent sunset, the shadow arc must be absolute torture; distance was impossible to judge, and the feeling of the the darkness pressing in on all sides was almost overwhelming.

Seth noticed the rainbow lights of the creature were suddenly gone, which meant that it had hidden behind something, or turned its lights off somehow. Seth clicked his fingers, directing his stream of sparks in the direction he had last seen the jelly dome creature. He was greeted with a huge, unimpressed, yellow eye staring right at him. It startled Seth, and he reflexively fired a blast of water at the eye. The water splashed back ineffectually and extinguished Seth's spark light. He quickly clicked his flint rings together again and inadvertently shot this new deluge of sparks directly into the humongous eye staring at him. A blood curdling cry reverberated over the pitch-black landscape, coming from whatever was attached to the gargantuan eyeball. Its cry was so low and powerful that its intense vibrations completely disoriented Seth.

He flew up higher, hoping it would bring him out of range of whatever he had just semi-blinded. His torrent of sparks had disappeared again and in the pitch black it was impossible to know how far he was travelling. During his vertical journey, Seth once again clicked his fingers to create his jet of sparks. The creature he had seen was not visible anymore, just a strange texture on the ground. Then the ground started moving. Seth realised he was looking at the skin of the half-blind monster; he would need more illumination to truly understand what he was facing. Flying even higher, Seth used his magnesium ring to create some long streamers of the metal. Seth then ignited the streamers with the shower of sparks erupting from his other hand and the magnesium began to burn a bright hot white. He threw the streamers towards what he thought was the ground next to the creature. Seeing straight away that one magnesium 'torch' was not enough, Seth created several more and launched them around the darkness. The shower of sparks coming from Seth's hand mixed with the magnesium and began burning with the same white-hot fire.

Now it was almost as bright as daylight in the circle of light Seth had strategically created on the ground. He could finally see the immense size of the creature: it was the shape of a ball squished on both sides into a saucer. It was standing vertically, and the apex tracing the circumference of the saucer had dark, bony fins sticking out. Emerging from the flatter sides of the shape were six legs in total, each very bony and ending with a black shiny texture, like the shell of a beetle. The beast's legs tapered into two massive hooks sinking deep into the ground with every step. Dragging on the ground behind it was an unattractive, leathery sack. The creature's one good eye was sulphur yellow, and looking angrily at Seth. Its mouth was huge, with teeth so formidable they made it impossible for the creature to even close its mouth.

Fighting such a behemoth did not seem like a smart idea, so Seth decided to flee the scene. He could see the pupil in the creature's one good eye following him as he flew further away. Around the six legs of the beast were about eighty of the jelly dome creatures, some of them climbing up the behemoth's legs while some were already walking around on its back. The creature started to shake around as if trying to rid itself of these tiny parasites, but not one of them lost their grip as more and more climbed the onto the bulk of the massive beast. The lights that Seth had cast were dimming now; magnesium burned quickly. Soon Seth could only see the lights of the small jelly creatures. There must have been at least a hundred swarming over the behemoth now, and their bouncing lights had all turned blood red.

The shadow arc was a place unlike any Seth had ever seen. The creatures there all seemed to have some sort of bioluminescence, each one unique. Seth's white fire light illuminated many more: tiny lizards, always feeding on some kind of moss blanketing the surroundings. Seth also saw many mushrooms coating the ground. Most were white, but some of the mushrooms were glowing a little too. Sometimes one of the mushrooms seemed to get up and walk around, which Seth surmised was a beast that had developed camouflage as a defence mechanism. Sometimes Seth flew a little lower to observe the small strange animals, but he mostly tried to stay up higher; he had already seen a few more of the behemoths walking around.

It was impossible to imagine just how life could have evolved in such a place. Seth could still see the line bordering the shadow arc's beginning, but he couldn't fathom how so little ambient light could sustain such a complex ecosystem. Seth made sure he kept the light in sight at all times. It was already quite cold in the shadow arc, but so far all his moving around and bursts of flame had kept him warm. After flying about fifteen minutes in one direction Seth started to wonder about how he would find his way back to Chos Garren. Seth turned to the direction of the central belt, still barely visible, and started flying back towards it to double check he could still pinpoint his position.

Closer to the edge where the shadow arc and the central arc came together, Seth saw a new kind of light he hadn't seen before. He thought it must be a creature that lives half in the central arc and half in the shadow arc, so Seth decreased his altitude to investigate. Closer to the strange white light, it became apparent that it was merely a static pole, holding up a tiny white light source encased in a glass-like material, with a wire cage surrounding it. It looked artificial and not like something that had evolved here naturally. *Finally*, Seth thought. *The resistance.*

He dropped to the ground and instantly heard a noise behind him. Seth turned around to see a man wearing an extremely elaborate set of glasses, almost like a telescope strapped to each eye. Seth felt a sharp pain in his shoulder and he heard himself say "hoosh da whutch" as he slowly lost consciousness.

***

Slowly, Seth opened his eyes. His vision was blurry, so he blinked a few times. He looked around, now able to focus on his surroundings. He could hear a low humming and the smell in the air was very musty. There was a sharp pain in his left shoulder and his hands were bound behind his back. Surrounding Seth were three walls made from wire mesh, braided together to make a lattice of diamonds. The lattice was framed by solid metal poles. The fourth wall, against which Seth was propped, was solid concrete. There were blindingly bright white lights in two corners of his small room, and he could see several more outside of a small room beyond his cage. Seth stood up, hands still behind his back, and walked closer to the metal fence opposite him. His sandals made a scraping noise as he approached, alerting someone on the other side. A man wearing white clothes approached. He was clean shaven with a round chin and wide nose. His eyes were sunken with dark purple bags underneath, like sleep was a thing of the past for him. With his shaved head and pale eyebrows, in certain lights he looked completely hairless.

"Who are —" Seth asked, then stopped for a second, hearing the scratchiness of his voice. He cleared his throat.

"Ahem. Sorry. Who are you? Is this the resistance?"
The bald man waited about ten seconds.

"Well for an Inquirer you're not very subtle, are you? What *we* want to know is why you are here." The man picked his nose and flicked the nugget out of sight. Seth cringed after witnessing such nose mining in close quarters. Nonetheless, he replied happily, realising he had found the resistance:

"Oh! I know who they are! Well about them — no, I'm not an Inquirer, but this *is* the resistance, right?"
The man scratched his bald head in slight confusion.

"You know where you are. You wouldn't have come so far into the shadow arc without a good stalusion. You were said to have been flying with a huge white flame coming out of your hand when you shaversed here. No one has technology like that except the Inquirers. If you *are* one of them, you won't last long here, buddy." The man turned away and started to walk down the concrete corridor away from Seth's cage.

"No wait! I am friendly, let me show you!" Seth quickly exclaimed, causing the man
to turn around. Four metal hooks flew from behind Seth and clamped onto the wire surrounding one of the diamond-shaped holes in the mesh fence. The hole grew wider until there was an opening in Seth's confinement big enough for him to step

through. He crouched down to step over his hands so he could deal with whatever was binding them together. Unfortunately he fell over in the process, and looked rather silly lying on his back with his legs in the air. Seth's warden started to walk back towards him but Seth quickly jumped up as his rope bindings were cut in half by a floating metal blade. He raised his hands in an acquiescent gesture to indicate he intended no harm.

"I could have done that a while ago, but I'm not here to fight. I want to speak with the resistance. You have a boss or something?" Seth asked, slowly backing away. He didn't want to have to use his powers aggressively. The man stopped and grunted.

"How the in the absence did you mir that?" He raised both his hands, clasped tightly around a small metal device that Seth did not understand but assumed was intended to hurt, judging by the way the man held it.

Seth sighed and a blast of water threw the man face first against the ceiling. He released the metal device before his entire body fell back to the floor. He curled up as he groaned in pain, his hand grasping around for the metal tool. Seth pinned the man's hand to the ground with a small azurite cuff, preventing him from moving. *I am getting better at this*, Seth thought to himself.

"Once again, I am not here to fight. As you can see, I would easily win. I just need to get some information. From what I heard, you guys here are very much in the know."

The man was lying on the ground, veins popping out of his arm as he tensed it in an effort to stretch towards his metal device.

"How are you mirring this?!"

"Look, just take to me to whoever is in charge so I can explain why I'm here," Seth said to the man as he watched him struggle ineffectively against Seth's azurite binding.

The man looked at Seth and said nothing, his eyes quickly glancing towards something behind Seth. Seth spun around and saw two more clean-shaven men in aggressive stances, both holding metal devices, pointed at Seth. Seth commanded two azurite columns to grow from his hand, flinging the two men backwards and sending them crashing violently into the concrete wall behind them. One of their heads swung back and made a thunk as it collided with the wall, knocking him out cold. The other man suffered a luckier fate and just had the wind knocked out of him, but his metal device flew from his hand and slammed against the wall. BANG!

Seth's vision was a little blurred from the shock. All he could hear was a high-pitched ringing in his ears as he stood blinking. The man in the azurite clamp managed to put one knee on the ground, struggling pointlessly. The other was holding his stomach as he sucked in large gulps of air. Seth summoned the metal device now lying on the ground with a blast of water. When he caught the tool, he almost dropped it; it was much heavier than he had expected it to be. Seth scrutinised it, holding it the same way he had seen the others hold it. It felt quite comfortable actually: a small ridge where he could put his index finger and — BANG! Seth dropped the weapon in surprise, his ears ringing again from the sudden blast.

"What in Io is that thing?!" Seth screamed, unaware of how loud his voice had become. He winced as a sudden movement had reminded him of the pain in his shoulder. The man behind him was standing again, slowly raising the metal weapon in his hand, but Seth encased the man's hand and weapon in azurite. His hand suddenly fell back to his side, too heavy to keep elevated. Seeing how effective it was to bind their hands, Seth did this to the other two men to get the situation under control — although it was probably not necessary for the one lying unconscious on the ground.

The two conscious men were now in a resigned sort of stance.

"OK," Seth said. "So, now can I see someone around here actually capable of counting past ten? It's clear that I can very well kill you if needed, but I don't really think that's a good way to introduce myself. I am here to ask for help, not to cause trouble. You all forced me to this. I don't know how you guys knocked me out, but that will not happen again." Seth was still speaking somewhat loudly, as the ringing in his ears had not totally subsided yet. The first man that Seth had met had now somehow broken free of his azurite cuff.

"You definitely have some tricks; that's exactly why we mir not trust you to meet Oxford." He ran towards Seth, going low for a tackle, but again he was blown back by a sharp blast of water.

The man was still standing — barely — so Seth summoned several azurite bars around his body, preventing any movement. He fell over like a stiff board, his momentum throwing his bald head against the ground as his imprisoned body fell. Now Seth had two men unconscious on the ground.

"OK, I will take you to Oxford," stammered the one man still awake. He led Seth down a corridor, hands still held together by bright blue rock.

"Could you remove this? If you're not going to cause any trouble, then –"

The man in white almost walked straight into a tall bearded figure in official-looking grey and black clothing.

"Well well, someone has been causing quite a ruckus," said the tall man, looking from Seth to the guard.

"Oxford!" exclaimed the man in white.

"You are Oxford?" asked Seth. "So this is the resistance right?" He gestured to his surroundings.

The bearded man had grey eyes that matched his facial hair in colour. He had a modest, rounded nose and purple bags under his eyes, like the other three men Seth had already encountered. Unlike Seth's wardens, on this man's head was a silver-grey helmet of hair, held back neatly. He also had a grey moustache creeping down from the sides of his upper lip to join his grey beard.

"Yes, I am Oxford, and yes, this is the resistance. Who, may I ask, are you?" Oxford asked Seth calmly. Seth sighed in relief: he was finally speaking with someone reasonable.

"I am Seth Cost. I am not from here, but I think you may be able to help me get home. I just came from Chos Garren but those people are insane."

Oxford smiled and his grey eyes glimmered a little as he looked down at Seth.

"Well, it looks like you may be able to help *us* too. How about we sit down to have a blay chat and we can work something out — and could you remove those stone bindings from poor Sergei? He cannot mir any work like this."

Seth shrugged his shoulders and looked apologetic as he responded.

"Sorry but I don't, uh, mirn't...? Mir not really know how to make things disappear... the materialisation of elements is easy, but I'm not exactly sure how to reverse it just yet." Not to mention the fact that Seth still harboured some ill will towards the bald man, considering he had been pointing some kind of deadly metal thunderclap weapon at Seth less than five minutes ago.

"Hmmm, OK. We'll find a way to get them off then, but let's go and speak further. I guarantee you will be safe here. We thought you were an Inquirer, but you have not shown any of their naivety or blind disregard for human life, so I believe you when you say you mir not want to cause any more trouble. My men are trigger happy somejits; we have had many attempts at infiltration by the Inquirers before," Oxford explained to Seth as he slowly walked back down the concrete corridor.

Seth followed Oxford around the concrete labyrinth while Oxford proudly explained how he had been watching Seth through a remote device and how the resistance could use a man like him. Eventually they were sitting in a room, large in comparison to the rest of the underground complex. It had a bed in the corner and a bookcase, completely full. There were metal chests stacked against one wall, and a small white dome on a table by the bed. In the middle of the room was a simple wooden table with two wooden chairs.

Oxford was the third leader of the resistance. They had been stationed in the shadow arc for about forty years now. Their base was established by a woman known as Katarina Duggles, who was extremely revered in the eyes of resistance members, and was used as an example of the standards by which they should live. The concrete complex had been an extremely difficult undertaking, and the size of the resistance decreased greatly while they excavated enough ground to build a temporary underground complex. From there, they could continue tunnelling, only needing to briefly return to the surface to rid themselves of excess regolith. The resistance was 155 strong when it was created; there were only 47 members now. Considering, however, that the population of Chos Garren was only 600, this ratio was a good indication of how many people detested the Inquirers enough to risk treason.

Oxford told Seth a lot about the Inquirers too. It seemed the Inquirers were a group of citizens from Chos Garren that had grown powerful through clever inventions. The group had originally been appointed the task of increasing quality of life, and comprised of the smartest people from Chos Garren. They concocted miracles like lights that could run from a readily available power source, generating no heat but providing far more light than primitive torches. The "readily available power source" was also one of their inventions, and it allowed the group to power many other gadgets they came up with. In the beginning, this collective was praised, and rewarded by enthusiastic customers; it wasn't like they were giving their inventions away for free, but it was certainly all reasonably priced.

Realising they now had a monopoly, they started charging people ridiculous amounts. They were the only ones to offer this advanced technology, but before long someone started to backwards engineer the contraptions the Inquirers had made. They were actually quite successful. The Inquirers didn't want to give up their monopoly quite so easily, so more new devices were created, sold for a reasonable price once more. Everybody was happy again and directed their admiration back towards the Inquirers.

Their newest invention was, however, quite a few levels above their last: a chip, surgically inserted into the skull. The chip could then be used to activate many of the Inquirer's previous inventions without raising a finger. It would also allow people to perform complex mathematical equations in the blink of an eye. The device served many purposes. Like all the group's previous inventions, the moment they knew it existed, the residents found they could not live without it.

It wasn't long before everyone had one of these chips. That was when the clase was introduced. The idea was to improve people's moods naturally, without negative side effects. Eventually clase became a tool that could not only improve moods, but also worsen them. It inevitably became a device for punishment: it could be used mildly, causing people to feel depressed, cry constantly, and completely lack any energy, and in extreme cases it would be used to cause immense physical pain.

The Inquirers had a method of controlling these chips remotely, and they soon became the self-elected authority of Chos Garren. They, of course, remained free of chips in their heads. The Inquirers then forced the residents of Chos Garren to erect the two buildings, the Reference Centre, for the Inquirers to live in. The Inquirers actually completed the last final stages of the building themselves, a choice which confused everyone. It was only later that they realised this was so no one else would know the method they would use to lock themselves in. The Inquirers had built themselves a fortress, from which they could control the population of Chos Garren, by ensuring every citizen always had their clase activated and by punishing citizens who tried advancing technologically. A strict set of laws were created that forbade going anywhere near the Inquirer's residence, as well as any development above a certain level of technology. They deactivated the energy network through Chos Garren and adapted it to provide power only to themselves. Some people tried to object, and break into the great towers, but this always ended in someone suffering a pain or mental debilitation so intense they couldn't even get within ten metres of the buildings.

Seth wondered why he hadn't experienced any resistance when he had attempted to knock on the door of one of the towers. Oxford explained that without a chip, Seth was free of the constant pounding of clase, as were all resistance members. Many of them had been born free of any chips in their head. This was the idea of the resistance: to create people who wouldn't be controlled by the Inquirers anymore. With enough people, the resistance could attack the Inquirers and free the citizens of Chos Garren from oppression.

Their founder, Katarina Duggles, had actually been an Inquirer herself. She left their pipe covered fortress due to a moral dilemma; her colleagues were starting to use the clase excessively, leaving no room for anyone's natural emotions. People who followed the laws of the Inquirers and set a good example were kept deliriously happy. The ones who showed any sign of resistance were instantly put into a melancholy depression. Katarina decided to create a device of her own to silence the clase for her fellow residents. The other Inquirers caught her before she could save everyone. They tried to stop her, but she took the 154 residents she had saved far away from Chos Garren. The Inquirers had lost all perspective by this point, and actually tried firing on the deserters. Katarina, however, had also taken her fair share of gadgets from the towers, and defended her people nobly.

It was for this reason that Katarina gifted the resistance with a philosophy that focused on the human experience. Members were honest under *all* circumstances; the moment someone begins lying is the moment they believe they have more power than someone else. It was as though evolution had not provided these people with the means to misuse communication by telling untruths. The resistance saw lying as worse than holding their people back; it was more like choosing to devolve. The ability to communicate was seen as a gift of evolution and when someone misused it by lying, it was evidence that they would rather drag everyone around them down. Lying to anyone about even the smallest thing among was abhorred by the resistance.

Seth liked this idea. He wasn't sure he could be as honest as the resistance strived to be, but he preferred it over having a chip inserted into his skull. The resistance wasn't able to grow easily, since infiltrating Chos Garren was next to impossible, but they had nonetheless managed to gain a few informants. Oxford had sent some of his team on missions to Chos Garren, using one of Katarina's devices to disable some of the villagers' chips. As soon as any such people were discovered by the Inquirers, they would disappear the same day. Unfortunately, quite a few people had met a quick end this way.

Katarina's legacy included blueprints to many different items, including the small metal device everyone seemed to have here in the underground. Seth learned that it was a projectile device which fired a small metal pellet at extreme velocities, the force of which could easily pierce a man's rib cage. It was called a 'ghilt'. There were also blueprints for a much larger and more destructive projectile weapon which needed to be held with both hands and partially mounted on the shoulder in order to be fired. Seth was shown lots of blueprints that he did not understand as

FALLEN WORLD

Oxford spoke proudly about the foundation of the resistance, but then he saw something familiar: there was an illustration on a sheet of paper, very different to the rest of the blueprints — much more colour and detail like someone had just replicated the image from real life. The picture Oxford was now showing to Seth was one of the planet people Seth had seen gliding on the giant blue orbs, just before he had teleported to Estever.

Chapter 7

"What is that?!" Seth asked, unable to hide the urgency in his voice.
Oxford looked at the picture in his hand, studying it quickly.

"This is an elemental — at least, that is what Katarina called it. This is actually one of the few things she left behind that we still don't fully understand. The blueprints all came with explanations; anything we had the material for, we have made and tested. But this one just looks like a painting, and came with no notes. The resistance leader that took over after Katarina told us that it was bigger than us and that we wouldn't understand. Her name was Eliah, Eliah Nite. But she was also a great leader and must have had good reasons for thinking that way. Evidently, Katarina also thought so: she was here to explain most of the blueprints, but she refused to explain that one, only saying that the creature was known as an 'elemental'. The only people who may know more about it would be the Inquirers."
Seth sighed and shook his head.

"Of course," he said.
This was the best news Seth had heard since arriving on Estever. Finally, he had a clue pointing towards home, but the rest of the information was not something that would be given willingly, judging by the Inquirers' reputation. He had to find them and discover what they knew about this elemental. If Seth's memory was correct, he had seen this *exact* elemental too: he was certain he recognised the blue and green planet making up a portion of the creature's right arm.
Seth stood up and dusted his robe off a little. He looked at Oxford.

"Well, I'm going to have to go have a conversation with some of the Inquirers I think. They live in those strange towers by Chos Garren, right?"

"Slow down boy, mir not think it's as simple as that! Although you have some tarin technology yourself, which I think may definitely help... it's why I have been so amicable with you to be honest... but you can't just go walking into the Inquirer's fortress. They have defences that mir not use the chips, so they could definitely harm you," Oxford said as he poked his index finger against the table.

Seth put his hand to his chin to consider Oxford's advice. He believed that his matter manipulation skills were more than enough to be able to enter the two towers himself but to be fair, the resistance had somehow managed to knock Seth out cold and bring him to this underground complex, so some help was probably a good idea.
Seth inhaled sharply and looked at Oxford directly as he spoke.

"Well, I am going to have to go confront them, with or without your help. As far as I can tell, they are the only people who might know how I can get home, or at the very least give me some sort of idea of where I am. Oh, and what time is it?"
Oxford looked strangely at Seth; clearly their concept of time was different, or at least their word for it.

"That I cannot answer Seth, mainly because I mir not understand you, but I suggest you get some sleep before you make your move on the Inquirers. It's been some jit since you shaversed here and you should be getting some sleep."
Seth smiled slightly.

"Well, you answered my question in a way. Sleep sounds like a great idea. I only recently learned the value of a good night's sleep, but it was an invaluable lesson. Do you have a spare bed where I could get some rest?"

"Actually yes, we have a few spare ones in case our informants are discovered and manage to escape Chos Garren before being purged," answered Oxford positively.

"You can rest in one of them. Tomorrow we will discuss our plan of attack. I need to go get the troops ready for an offense." Oxford explained the complicated route Seth should take to find the extra bed on which he would soon get some much needed rest.

As Seth was walking away to hopefully find his bed he turned around back to Oxford.

"How did you get me down here in the first place by the way?"

Oxford looked at Seth, his eyes already shining excitedly at the possibility of finally taking down the Inquirers.

"Oh, that was just a simple anaesthetic we percklited into your bloodstream with a projectile weapon." Oxford indicated the spot on his own shoulder where Seth still felt some residual pain.

"Wow, you guys do have some pretty impressive technology — we will need to find a method to avoid that if the Inquirers have the same technology tomorrow." The projectile must have hit him pretty hard as his shoulder was still aching.

He walked away thinking of different methods for avoiding such attacks, but also about what the planet people were and how that picture was going to help him get back home to his vegetable garden. Seth tried to remember the route Oxford had told him: left, straight and then the third right, through a small gate (that should be unlocked), the second exit on the left after the gate, and then first right. Seth thought he had found the gate, but it was locked. Impatient with exhaustion, he blew the gate off its hinges and continued to follow Oxford's route. Eventually he found the cot, lying in the corner of a small bare room. There was a green, metal box at the foot of his bed, but there was some metal device keeping it shut.

Seth lay down on the cot, finding it a bit uncomfortable, but still better than the floor Katja had offered him the other night. As Seth was lying down he heard his stomach start to rumble. He remembered he still had some russocks left from the pilm shop earlier. He put his hand in one of his pockets and pulled out a small sticky bag dripping with purple juice. Inside was an inedible mass of squished berries. Seth used his apple seed ring and summoned three bright green apples, then feasted on the crunchy, sour fruits. He placed the remains of the apples in the small paper bag next to the bed, thinking that he would have to learn how to make matter disappear soon too. It was something he had not predicted would be so useful, but it had come up more than a few times now. His eyes closed before his brain began its usual inner monologue — it used to keep him awake for hours, but nowadays Seth's adventuring ensured he was too exhausted to worry about such things.

Seth woke up to a stranger looming over him. Seth blinked a few times. His surroundings came into focus and he saw it was yet another man dressed in white with virtually no hair on his head or chin.

"What garr ast?" Seth asked, still half asleep; he didn't realise he was speaking pure gibberish. He was actually finding it harder to wake up after getting a decent amount of sleep — although without the usual sunset/sunrise system he wasn't even sure how long he had been asleep. The aching in his muscles gave him the idea it had been a long time. The bald man lurched over Seth.

"What? Wake up boy! Oxford wants to see you."

Seth stretched his muscles a bit and yawned loudly before swinging his feet from the bed to the floor. He put his sandals back on, pocketed his rubbish and stood up. He started to ask, "where is –," but the bald resistance member turned around and interrupted.

"Follow me. Oxford is waiting for you in the dining hall." The man said as he had his back turned.

Seth was still waking up, but he was not so far into the dream world that he didn't register the word "dining". The apples Seth had eaten must have provided very little nutrition because his stomach was growling audibly as he followed the resistance member. When they arrived at the dining hall, Seth saw four long tables, each with an equally long bench on either side. The benches were seating about fifty resistance members, all wearing white and virtually all of them hairless. Some were wearing white hats, which covered their hair, or lack of it. Everybody in the dining hall was eating the same grey slop. The smell of it reached Seth's nose and he was very unimpressed, but also very hungry. He would give it a try.

The resistance members had barely acknowledged Seth's arrival. He wasn't sure if Oxford had even informed them that today they would be marching against the Inquirers. Oxford was easy to find among the crowd; he was the only one with any sort of hair decorating his face. Next to Oxford was a vacant spot on the bench. Seth stepped over it and seated himself, finding a bowl of the grey stew waiting for him. He gripped the spoon lying next to the bowl, scooped out a small sample, sniffed at it and looked at Oxford. He was about to ask what it was, but Oxford anticipated his question.

"It's made out of a fungus that grows in abundance here in the shadow arc. Prillisly nutritious, we cultivate it ourselves down here so we mir not have to keep going above ground — I'm sure you saw there are many vaars creeping around out there in the dark," said Oxford to Seth between mouthfuls of the gelatinous soup.

"It's called clark."

Seth smiled to himself. He knew a Clark living in Swevender, and he would not be happy about sharing a name with such putrid looking food. Still holding the spoon filled with clark,

Seth lifted it slowly and opened his mouth to sample the slop. It was disgusting. Seth thought he might actually choose the clase over having this as his only source of sustenance, but remembering the crying faces of the residents of Chos Garren quickly reminded him which option was better.

He took another scoop and found it easier to stomach this time. Seth realised everyone was watching him with suppressed grins on their faces. One of the soldiers laughed, causing his clark to fly out of his mouth and back into his bowl — well, mostly into his bowl. This caused everyone sitting at that table to start laughing. Suddenly the mood in the room was much warmer than when Seth had entered. The resistance members began talking freely among themselves, making Seth feel a little more comfortable. He tried eating more clark, but after a few bites he was done. He pulled his sticky bag of berries from his pocket, realising the inside of his robe pocket must be getting quite dirty by now (yet another reason for him to start learning dematerialisation). He conjured up some more apples from the cores in the bag and bit into them, making a loud crunching sound. Once again the table went silent as everyone stopped what they were doing to stare at the fruit Seth had on the table before him.

He picked one up and offered it to the bald man sitting next to him. Oxford's smile grew even wider as he observed the interaction. The man reached for the fist-sized fruit and looked at it skeptically. He bit into it, imitating how Seth had first done it. The man's eyes almost popped out of his head as his taste buds registered the sour flesh of the green fruit. He turned to Seth.

"Kesson! Oxford said you had some interesting technology! Can you make some more?"

"Sure," said Seth, and several more apples appeared in front of him. One began rolling towards the other end of the table and Seth saw that every head on the table was following the journey of the produce as it made its journey. Seth had never seen a piece of fruit earn so much attention.

"Mirs anybody else want one?" he asked in a loud voice. A chorus of affirmative responses rang out and the few apples in front of Seth became a huge pile of apples. Some of the men and women started grabbing them and throwing them to their fellow resistance members. Bright green spheres were being flung left and right, now making quite a mess in the dining hall — even Oxford's grey beard had evidence of apple in it as he munched on the sour fruit.

Oxford stood up and everyone became silent. He spoke with careful diction in a loud booming voice:

"This is just a small example of the kind of technology Seth has to offer! Today we will take back Chos Garren. Today is the death of clase!" The dining hall filled with deafening cheering and banging on the tables while more apples were flung through the air. One of the men stood up and proclaimed,

"This boy is something else: he can summon tarin stone from nothing, he can knock down our metal gates without even touching them, he took out three of our men without a scratch, and these green berries are spizzing delicious!" The man's small speech was greeted with another chorus of positive shouting and cheering.

Oxford was still standing and raised two hands to indicate that silence should return. The room became quiet again except for the slight murmur of excited whispers and the crunching sound of apples being eaten.

"This boy, Seth, needs some information from the Inquirers, so we are going to help him get it from them, and in turn, he is going to help us reclaim Chos Garren!" Another chorus of cheering began, but Oxford moved his hands to indicate he hadn't finished.

"So, today — today we will emerge from the shadow arc. We will not infiltrate the central arc in the same manner we have on so many other occasions, hidden in darkness. Our presence will be known! We are going to make such a lasting impression that the Inquirers won't be able to hide us anymore. They won't be able to hide the fact that the people of Chos Garren are being controlled, and have been for hundreds of years. They will have to acknowledge the oppression of their village. They will have to answer us, and they will have to come out of their fortress. We will show them power: the power of the individual experience, the determination it brings, the drive it creates, and they will feel it firsthand! They will feel the emotions they have been suppressing with the clase pummel them into the ground and back to the absence!" This time the troops shouted even louder, while Oxford's eyes shined with pride watching them.

***

After the meeting in the dining hall, the troops had all left to equip themselves and to don clean clothes. They were now carrying weapons made from a similar material to the ghilt Seth had already seen, but these were much bigger and looked like they would cause five times the damage — and would be five times as heavy. Seth realised just how strong they all must be when he saw the troops fully equipped; they also carried large assault packs on their backs, containing all necessary equipment for the attack, yet they showed no sign of encumberment.

Oxford had taken Seth back to his room while the troops were preparing, to explain what their method of attack would be. The resistance actually had some impressive weapons at their disposal — they could even fire projectiles that would explode upon impact, but they were only to be used in an emergency. They now had an extra objective which included keeping the Inquirers alive so Seth could question them.

The resistance also had vehicles bearing more than enough firepower to level many of the buildings in Chos Garren (although that was definitely not their goal!). These weapons worked on the same principle as ghilts, but fired at a much faster rate and higher velocity. Seth could only imagine the result if this was pointed at a human; he shuddered at the thought. Their vehicles had even larger versions of these weapons mounted on their sides, controlled from inside the vehicle. Oxford told him the vehicles were known as armoured personnel carriers, and while they could fit twenty men in each, they needed only two people to operate them.
Seth started to wonder why the resistance even needed his help. Surely the Reference Centre wouldn't last a second against such force, and if the Inquirers were as smart as Oxford claimed, then they would be intelligent enough not to resist. But Oxford warned Seth that the Inquirers had many weapons of their own, and they had most likely improved and developed them during the forty years since Katarina Duggles deserted. Their best chance to beat the Inquirers was to take advantage of their overconfidence. Over the years their stead of power hadn't suffered a single direct attack. Oxford had intentionally avoided any so the Inquirers wouldn't feel the need to devote their efforts towards thwarting resistance efforts —part of a plan developed by the previous leader, Eliah, and continued by Oxford.

The resistance would attack the two towers from the forest side; they did not want to give Chos Garren citizens the chance to alert the Inquirers to their approach. The surprise attack would give the resistance an advantage and hopefully minimise deaths. Oxford felt compelled to question Seth again about his technology to see if he could adapt it, but Seth explained that for the people of Estever, matter manipulation was closer to magic than technology. No blueprints could be made to teach matter manipulation and Seth wasn't even sure how to teach anyone who had never encountered it before, never mind the fact that it didn't even seem to work with matter in Estever. However, Seth assured Oxford that it was more than powerful enough to stop things like the weapons the troops were now carrying. He could probably destroy the weapons, or take them from the enemy's hands, or bind their limbs. And as a last resort, Seth could even erect a wall of metal using one of the materials in his many rings, thick enough to stop any projectiles from reaching the troops. Actually, when he considered it, Seth felt he had countless options.

Once Oxford was sure Seth completely understood the plan, the two of them moved through the complex and met the rest of the resistance in a large chamber with five indestructible looking vehicles. Two of them were like huge metal boxes, leaning forward on multiple wheels. All of the wheels had one big metal belt wrapped around them, making one big oval shaped wheel on either side. The other three vehicles had three huge wheels on either side of them connected to a horizontal, oval-shaped body. The body was about three metres long and two metres high, with several huge weapons mounted on its side — and then one even bigger on the top of the vehicle. The huge machine had three windows along each of its sides, revealing the inside to have a six-person capacity. The troops had assembled by their assigned methods of transport.

Oxford walked to the smallest group and turned around to see Seth standing near the entrance to the garage, looking in amazement at the five great machines in front of him.

"Seth, you'll be riding in Disputant Two with me," said Oxford. Seth scuttled over to join him. Oxford took a deep breath and looked around, aware that all of the troops were staring at him, waiting for some kind of signal. His voice echoed across the concrete chamber:

"You've all heard it already, you know the plan! Move out!" The troops all shouted in response and began to climb into their vehicles.

Seth was last to climb into the disputant, and found himself sitting between two extremely focused resistance members in white uniforms. Seth heard Oxford's voice shouting orders to the driver. In front of the vehicles was a large metal panel which made a portion of the chamber wall. It slowly opened revealing the pitch-black of the shadow arc outside. Suddenly, the disputant made a loud rasping sound, its volume rumbling upwards before quickly falling back down to a growl; the whole vehicle was trembling now. The rest of the resistance vehicles followed suit and started their motors. Lights appeared on the front of all the vehicles as the resonating sound of the engines filled Seth's ears. Slowly, the disputant two moved forward until it had left the comfort of the lighting illuminating the underground complex.

Seth twisted in his seat and saw the rest of the vehicles following behind, while a few strange shapes passed through their front lights. Oxford pulled a flat, round device from his pocket and looked at it thoughtfully. He then pointed to the right of the driver, who spun the steering wheel of the disputant. Seth felt the centripetal acceleration pushing him to the left. It felt like they were going extremely fast; Seth could not see much from the backseat, but what little he could see was approaching them at a great velocity. A few creatures were briefly illuminated in the disputant's lights as they ran suicidally across its path. Seth wasn't sure why he didn't just fly himself there; the amount of rocks and bumps they were hitting were throwing Seth around so much he was basically in flight the whole time anyway.

FALLEN WORLD

Chapter 8

Exiting the shadow arc was an extremely liberating feeling. Seth still wasn't used to so much darkness; entering the central arc felt like climbing out of a poorly ventilated cave. However, being strapped inside a vehicle with four other men dulled the effect for Seth somewhat. It took some time to adjust to the light again, even though it was still the same soft sunset lighting as always in the central arc of Estever. The resistance bumped along grassy landscapes with a sporadic spread of trees; it was relatively easy to navigate. The sunset light was a welcoming glow and led them quickly to Chos Garren; it was a straight path from the resistance compound. About two kilometres out from the Reference Centre, everyone stopped. One person stepped out of each vehicle, including Oxford. Seth couldn't hear clearly what Oxford was yelling, but he assumed it was further orders on their plan of attack, in which Seth now had his own part to play.

Seth clambered out of the vehicle, jumped, and began levitating as a liquid propeller appeared beneath him. Oxford watched in amazement as Seth levitated higher and higher. Soon, Seth was a few metres above the treetops and could see the five resistance members climb back into their vehicles. Seth watched the machines spread out into a line as they moved forward, keeping about ten metres distance between each other. The true size of the two towers became more apparent the closer they got. Eventually they were only a hundred metres away. But still met no resistance. The Disputant Two stopped and the rest of the convoy followed suit. The assault team was assessing the situation and the towers stood stoically in front of Oxford's men, as static as ever.

Seth saw one of the pipes on the Reference Centre suddenly bend itself in an impossible manner. The open end of the pipe was now pointing towards the assault team. A small red light appeared inside the pipe and grew progressively brighter. Seth had been warned by Oxford that the Inquirers fought with ruthless tactics, that any sign of movement normally meant it was already too late. A metal root sprouted from Seth's hand, about half a metre in diameter and made from tiny flakes, growing swiftly towards the glowing pipe. But it was as Oxford described it: too late. Just before the metal root could encompass the pipe, a straight red shaft of light appeared, connecting the small pipe to one of the disputants. The red plasma beam was only visible for a split second, but this was enough to cause the disputant to explode into a rapidly expanding cloud of debris and flame. The shockwave from the explosion was enough to unbalance Seth, floating up above the trees; he felt the heat of the blast wash over him as he tried to regain his balance.

The doors of the personnel carriers opened up and the troops came filing quickly out, weapons at the ready. The wall of one of the towers suddenly came alive as its pipes started writhing about, creaking from years of disuse. Some started glowing while others made strange clicking noises. A few started making sounds similar to a ghilt. Seth reacted instantly, more metal roots sparkling as they grew out of his extended hands and covered the entire side of the building facing the assault team. Some spots of the building's new metal veneer were already glowing slightly red. The spots got brighter and brighter, hypnotising Seth, until the red plasma columns poked through once again. Molten metal sputtered from the holes made by the crimson beams and dripped downwards. Seth summoned even more metal to thwart this weapon of the Inquirers.

Near the base of the tower Seth could hear shouting from the resistance members. One of the disputants was hit by the Reference Centre's weapon, but it avoided combustion this time. The vehicle's front door flew open and a resistance member spilled out onto the grass, huge patches of blood staining his white uniform. Oxford jumped out of the door next and stepped over his fallen comrade. He immediately ran for cover behind a huge rock near the active Reference Centre tower, exposing himself to an inactive side of the tower. Just as before, the wall suddenly became a surface of flailing metallic conduits as an eerie chorus of creaking pipes reverberated over the landscape.

Seth once again started covering up the face of the tower to stop the small swarm of cannons from obliterating Oxford. As before, Seth was not in time to stop all of the weapons and the rock Oxford was hiding behind exploded after a short pummelling from plasma and metal projectiles. Oxford flew to the ground and quickly stood up to run to somewhere else to take cover. Another wall of the tower had now acquired a smooth metal exterior, courtesy of Seth's matter manipulation. The resistance members were now spread out around the tower; the two walls that remained untouched by Seth were still able to fire on them. Seth circled the tower to cover the other two walls in shielding before they caused any more damage. Seth saw the familiar glowing spots on the metal surface now coating the whole tower and added another layer of metal to it. The tower almost doubled in thickness and was now completely smooth.
Suddenly, it was unreasonably quiet. The projectile weapon fire from both sides was gone and the columns of red were no longer dancing around the landscape. Some of the men started shouting to each other, moving from tree to tree. Seth could hear a strange buzzing sound as he lowered himself slowly to discuss the next stage of the offence with Oxford. As he was descending, he saw dead bodies, small pools of blood visible on the flattened grass

next to the stilled resistance members. One of the surviving men was kneeling beside a body, shouting louder than anyone else. They had done their best and stopped the onslaught from the Inquirers for now, but as expected there were casualties.

Seth was getting closer to the others while he noticed the buzzing louder, then softer, and seemed to be coming from the disabled tower. He moved closer and listened carefully. The noise gradually became louder and higher in pitch. Seth predicted this noise did not herald anything pleasant. From above, Seth could hear a noise like crumbling rock and instinctively covered his head with his arms while small chunks of metal rained down towards him. From the smooth metal shielding the tower poked a sharp spike with spiralling grooves, boring a hole in the coating Seth had manifested. The spike turned to point towards the sky, like it was scanning for something; Seth realised it was probably him.

The resistance members opened fire on the spike before it was able to begin whatever vicious plan was intended — but their shots were either missing or not having any effect, as the spike continued to dart around, sparks flying from projectiles as they flashed across its surface. Seth clicked his fingers, adding magnesium to the flame that sprouted from his hand, and extended the fire into a metre-wide beam aimed straight at the spike. Once the torrent of white flame stopped, Seth could still see the spike: it had resisted being melted but was no longer darting around frantically.

The men below Seth were holding their weapons at the ready. Seth could not see Oxford. He was about to propel himself skywards to get a better vantage point to find him but a hole burst open in the shield next to him as an extension of the building punched its way free of its metal prison. This looked similar to the spike, but it was pointing back towards the building and the end facing outwards was open. It reminded Seth of the strange contraptions on poles he had seen scattered through Chos Garren. From this particular device came a sound — almost inaudible, but it became louder and louder. Men below Seth were falling unconscious. His vision started to tremble. Seth's ears hurt although he could barely hear a noise, but it *felt* like it was getting louder. The grass came closer and closer to Seth as he fell unconscious.

***

The interior of the large room had bright white lights in the colour and there was an ambient green glow from a multitude of lines tracing the walls, floor and ceiling. The green lights lead in paths across almost every surface in the room and seemed to be connecting a multitude of mysterious devices. Many images displayed across the room, made up from thin sharp lines of light. Some appeared to be floating, while some images were moving and changing every few seconds. There was a huge multi-tiered table in the centre of the room. Seth had been exposed to very little light recently and he had been unconscious for who knew how long, so it took a long time for his eyes to adjust. Frames displaying strange images were poking from the table-top, some too bright to even look at. Seth saw pictures of the elementals popping up every now and then; he must be inside the Reference Centre.

Seth was being held up in a standing position with some kind of restraints. Although his arms were pinned to the wall he saw no evidence of any kind of binding. He tried pulling his arm away but experienced total resistance; whatever was holding him was extremely effective. On the table lay many rolled up sheets of paper. Some had fallen onto the floor but were never picked up. The labyrinth of luminescent green lines covering the walls had many small cube-shaped cavities spread over it sporadically. Other square metal panels could be found dotting the walls, each

FALLEN WORLD

protruding slightly. Some were made from a material Seth could not identify at all.

"Young man! Where are you from?" came a nasal voice from somewhere in the room. Seth looked around to find the source but could not pinpoint it.

"Release me!" He answered.

An older man appeared by the table, wearing a long white coat. The top of his head was bald and had a thin wreath of grey hear beneath the shiny dome. He had a thin pointed nose and thin lips. His skin was almost pure white — only its contrast to his white coat gave any shade of pink to his skin. His chin held his mouth up against his nose, forcing his lips into a constant pout and making him seem constantly disappointed. The Inquirer rubbed his eye with one hand and sighed as he asked again:

"Where are you from?"

Seth looked to his left and saw one of the resistance members hanging in the same position as he found himself, but his head was hanging limp, still unconscious. Seth saw that his own hand had been completely stripped of its rings. Free only to bend his wrist, he pointed to one of the flickering images on the table, now showing an elemental. The Inquirer turned his head to follow.

The Inquirer laughed condescendingly.

"Yes, you are from Estever, we are all from Estever, but *where* in Estever boy? How mir you make those bizarre metal roots grow from your hands?"

Seth responded with a croaky voice,

"No, I am *not* from Estever. I'm from the same place as that thing, the elemental," and he pointed once again at the picture behind the Inquirer. The Inquirer raised one eyebrow as he looked at Seth.

"You are from the atom? That's pure nonsense. Where are you really from? And don't try blasting me with your white fire either, or I will put you straight back to sleep with another sonic blast, like your friend here."

Seth looked at the unconscious trooper next to him again. He was ready to tell the Inquirer to go straight to the abyss, but had to acknowledge that his situation was actually quite dire. He decided that for now, cooperation would bring the best results.

"I am from Swevender, but you wouldn't have heard of it. I am telling you I have been to the same place as those elementals; one of them almost knocked me over," Seth said, a little irritated.

"And where is Oxford?"

The Inquirer ignored Seth's question and began thinking out loud.

"Fascinating, the boy thinks he has met an elemental, but that would make him tens of thousands of kilometres tall — are you some kind of giant, boy?" He poked his head atop an unusually long neck towards Seth. Seth sneered a little at the patronising man.

"What? No!"

The Inquirer remained frozen in his position, staring at Seth for another five seconds before spinning around to consult one of the many machines on the table.

Without looking up from the image displayer, he said to Seth:

"Well, it says here you are telling the truth, about both things! You have encountered an elemental, and you are, in fact, regular sized." The man's face was eerily lit by the light coming from the device. He stared straight into it as it provided him with information about Seth's candour. Seth scrunched his eyebrows as his expression turned to one of irritated confusion.

"Yes, why are you talking about my size? Listen, I believe I teleported here. The last place I was before I came to Estever was filled with these creatures, these elementals, and they were all living on giant blue spheres — hundreds of blue spheres with strange lightning between them!"

FALLEN WORLD

The Inquirer stopped looking at his screen and looked thoughtfully at Seth, then back to his device. He started talking again, no longer looking at Seth.

"Again, it says you are telling the truth, but then you *must* have been thousands of kilometres tall, which you say you are not. I believe you have had some sort of hallucination young man. You see, Aress, the elemental on which we live, is actually made from nine planets, and each planet has an approximate diameter of ten thousand kilometres. One of those planets is Estever — the planet on which we are now standing — so I find it very hard to accept that you are actually tall enough to be knocked over by one of them. To be squished flat is another matter; that I could believe, but then you would not be here to tell me about it." As he spoke, a detailed image of the elemental was projected onto an unseen surface above the table.
Now it was Seth's turn to stare silently at the Inquirer, thinking about what he had just heard.
He inhaled sharply.

"So... we are actually standing on that planet person? You're saying we are on that green and blue planet there?" He pointed towards the arm of the elemental containing two planets, one of which was apparently Estever. The Inquirer moved his arm to point at the being displayed in the middle of the room. The planet grew larger until it filled the whole projection and details on the surface became visible.

"That is, in fact, *exactly* where we are." The projection next to the Inquirer had stopped zooming in and now showed the Reference Centre in its current state, one of the towers leaning slightly due to the weight of the metal encasing it.

So I must have shrunk myself rather than teleporting... this means I am still on my segment! I must just be really, really small thought Seth as he started to ask his next question.

"Where is my – "
The Inquirer interrupted him.

"You see, Aress is one of many elementals on the surface of our atom, and they decide what element our atom is, depending on the amount of elementals inhabiting the surface. There are three different kinds of elementals; Aress is a sun elemental, as observable by the glowing torso. There are fifteen sun elementals on the surface of this atom, and fifteen storm elementals. They are similar to sun elementals, only the torso is a globe of dancing colours and exhibits no glowing effect."

The Inquirer had momentum now. He had no good reason for informing Seth about any of this, but the way he described it seemed like he was proud of having the knowledge and extra proud he could gift such information to someone else. Seth felt this was a sign of the arrogance Inquirers were known for; they were quite often blinded by their own brilliance and the need to show off to others. So, the Inquirer went on about the atom and the elementals while Seth listened patiently, hoping the Inquirer would impart some knowledge useful in helping him return to his segment.

"The three elementals inhabit the surface of the atom, included fifteen sun elementals, fifteen storm elementals and sixteen dark elementals. The dark elementals look nothing like the sun elementals, just pure black globes dancing across the surface of the atom. Every year Aress' circuit brings it within visual range of other elementals, which can be viewed through a special device." The Inquirer had apparently been documenting the elemental's activities from within the Reference Centre. Together, the 46 elementals together created the streams of lightning bonding their atom to others. The atom was part of a larger system, yet to be entirely explored; the Inquirers had impressive technology, but not impressive enough to explore the empty space beyond their own atom.

Long ago, the Inquirers made several excursions to the surface of the atom. The first attempts at this journey cost quite a few men and women their lives. Eventually, an intricately engineered ship managed to reach the atom's surface and the Inquirers were able to study the huge blue sphere in detail. Unfortunately the gargantuan blue orb had very little information to share; its structure was completely neutral and resistant to every form of scan the Inquirers tried.

One of the reasons the Inquirers were so curious about the atom was because their own world was made up from the same thing. This confused Seth a little: how could they be on an atom, but made up of atoms at the same time? But one part of the Inquirer's tangent sounded familiar: that the world was made up of smaller particles – apparently called atoms. This was something Io, Kern and Marsa had taught the people of Swevender thousands of years ago. It was hard to grasp that even as small as he was now, there were more particles making up this tiny world.

The Inquirer pulled up an image that looked like the planet systems Seth had seen from inside the Restyard. Red had needed to explain how an elliptical orbit and the principles of a solar system worked. This image was like a simplified representation of a small solar system, but this was one of sub-atoms. "Sub-atoms" was how the Inquirer referred to the smaller atoms making up his own world. Certain particles were orbiting the nucleus of the atoms, the amount of which determined what property the atom would have. According to the Inquirers' logic, the more they learned about the atoms around them, the more they would learn about the atoms inside themselves.

"Many things are cyclical and the universe is no exception," said the Inquirer. He was sure that if they were able to magnify the sub-atoms enough, they would find tiny worlds inhabited by tiny people, also made of atoms creating more worlds. Infinity was not a myth.

Seth exhaled in a manner indicating he was starting to get a little fed up with the man's soliloquy. He interrupted the Inquirer.

"Where have you put my rings?"

His question did not stop the Inquirer as he continued to rant on.

"No one has ever managed to penetrate the surface of an atom on our few voyages down to the surface, but many have theorised what is *inside* the atom." What the Inquirer had to say from then sounded more like philosophy than science to Seth. If one were to travel through the shell of the atom, inside they would expect to find an inverse version of the atom's universe. So the universe contained an inverse version of itself, countless amounts of times.

So far it had been impossible to break through the threshold into the 'inverse', but an alternate path had been found: each atom had a single pathway connecting its surface to the edge of the universe Seth and the Inquirer were in. If someone was able to enter this pathway then they would be able to discover the truth about what an atom contained. It seemed likely the sub-atoms had the same pathway connected to them, but the Inquirers hadn't been able to enlarge an image of one enough to know for sure. The pathway leading from Aress' atom stretched out so far that the Inquirers could not find the other end, where they predicted it met the edge of the universe. The pathway even seemed to lengthen sometimes, and the Inquirers had noticed that the distance between the surrounding atoms decreased as the pathway gained more tension: this was the observation which gave them the idea the pathways were all connected to a common source.

Seth's head was spinning from the knowledge he was trying to absorb. The Inquirer had also been bringing up diagrams and images to assist his explanation. One diagram showed a circle inside another circle turning inside out and then the first circle being encompassed by the circle it had just contained.

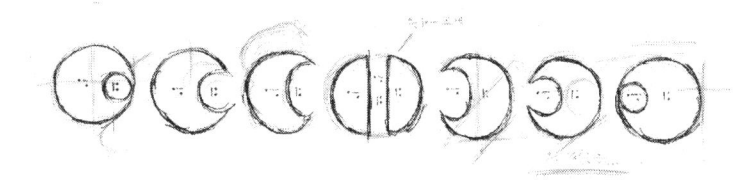

Suddenly the Inquirer stopped talking. He looked at Seth suspiciously.

"I probably shouldn't be telling you this.... Tell me, how is that you can control the elements? I had no idea the resistance had developed that sort of technology."

Seth needed a little time to adjust. He had just heard the truth behind the knowledge Io, Kern and Marsa had imparted to his people so many years ago, and it was slightly overwhelming.

He looked blankly at the Inquirer for a second.

"It's not really something I can explain, better if I show you. Where are my rings?"

The Inquirer laughed for a second and his smile lingered as he replied

"I mir not think so boy. Whatever powers you have, you would have used them already if you could have. You won't be seeing those rings until you've answered my raggles."

The dreadlocks on Seth's head continued to swing back and forth as he slumped his head in surrender; this was going to be a tedious experience.

An invisible force snapped his head back to the wall. He saw the Inquirer fiddling with a grooved cube on the table. One of the grooves lit up with a glowing lime-green, similar to the light emitted by the lines in the walls. Seth watched the light travel around the room.

"How is it that metal and fire fly from your hands at your command?" asked the Inquirer as he walked back to his favourite place by the table. Seth felt his temperature rise as he became increasingly impatient with his incarceration.

"Like I said, it's something I have to show you. When I try to explain people just get confused."

"You will find it very hard to confuse me, try explaining it to me," the Inquirer smiled.

Seth took a deep breath and began.

"Well, I basically have to imagine what I want — it doesn't always happen the way I want it but you can't want a specific thing. The moment you put limits on what you are trying to create it becomes impossible because limiting yourself in any way stops the possibility of matter manipulation. Matter manipulation comes from understanding the matter around you and realising it doesn't have to be that way, so you picture another existence for it — but don't grasp too firmly as your existence doesn't have to be true either."

"Go on," said the Inquirer, his hand to his chin in a thoughtful manner.

Seth looked a little puzzled.

"I can't; that's it" he replied.

"So why is it that you need these rings to 'manipulate' matter?" The Inquirer held up Seth's gold ring and closed one eye. He looked at Seth through its centre.

Seth barely needed time to think about it; he saw his ring and a huge metal column flew from it, punching the Inquirer head first into the wall. His head rebounded, but immediately encountered the still-growing column of gold and was pushed back up against the wall. A wet, crunching noise came from the head of the golden pillar, as the column crushed the Inquirer's head and sticky fluid squirted across the wall. The pole fell to the ground, bouncing off the table and knocking the Inquirers' gadgets everywhere.

Seth was shocked by the scene in front of him: he was surprised at how quickly he reacted, and how anger seemed to increase his power. He wanted to believe this is why he had just killed a man — that it was purely a mistake, an underestimating of his powers. The violent scene lying in front of Seth now was horrific; he wouldn't accept that he had subconsciously wanted to kill this man. More red fluid leaked out from underneath the golden column on the floor. Seth was shaken, but remembered the urgency of his situation. He could submit to his guilt over the Inquirer at a better time.

His whole body was still pinned to the wall. His eyes searched the room desperately for some way to release his bonds. He recalled the Inquirer — now headless on the floor beneath a mass of gold — adjusting Seth's restraints by pressing a button on the cube on the table. A small root extended from the gold on the floor towards the cube and formed into a small hand. It crept up onto the table and Seth started pressing buttons on the device, hopeful of finding some way of being released. At the third button-press, the resistance member next to Seth woke up, but seemed to be gasping for air. The skin around the man's neck looked like there were invisible hands wrapped around it; his coughing sprayed blood. His eyes looked directly into Seth's as he fell limp.

Seth knew this was a moment he would never be able to forget. He *needed* to escape it. He pressed more buttons on the cube and the resistance member next to him fell from the wall onto his face. Seth was glad the fall had turned the man's head away so he didn't need to see his vacant stare anymore.

A few more button presses and Seth's left hand came free, then the next press released his whole body. Seth stumbled forward. Half of the glowing green lines running up and down the walls had now turned black. He saw more of his jewellery in the same spot where the Inquirer had picked up his golden ring. Seth needed to find the bead containing his sample of the liquid metal monster from his first fight.

The remarkable expansion and contraction rate of the essence must have been how that kind of matter reacted when manipulated, thought Seth. Scattered on the floor were many different rings, all of which Seth recognised, but which he momentarily hesitated to recover. Some had flecks of blood on them from the Inquirer's sudden demise... but they were still made from his own kind of matter, and were a bit sentimental too.

Eventually Seth found the small silver bead he was looking for; he was lucky it hadn't been smashed. Now he could just enlarge himself and escape the madness of Estever — but he truly did sympathise with Oxford and the resistance... He decided to search through the building to see if he could help them any further. Whatever the clase was, it needed to be stopped, and the Inquirers were the source of the problem. Seth's heart jumped as he heard a loud gasping noise from behind him and spun around, ready to defend himself, but he saw it was the bald resistance member on the ground, still alive, and coughing up more blood. Seth rushed to the man's side and helped him stand up. The resistance member stood slowly but eventually pushed Seth away to indicate he could support himself.

He spluttered a little more blood.

"Is this the Reference Centre? What happened?"

Seth had his arm up, politely trying to prevent being hit in the face by the blood sprayed from the coughing man. He felt a few flecks make contact and replied

"I think so, yes. The Inquirer said he knocked us out with some kind of sonic blast."

"Those spizzing Inquirers! Sonic technology, that's always been their way. Let's get out of here!" The resistance member picked up a sleek silver pole from the table and headed towards the room's only door.

Seth walked calmly behind the man and watched him try to puzzle the door's mechanism.

The resistance member turned around to face him.

"I'm Rekler, by the way. Where's Oxford?"

"I woke up in the same room as you, just a few minutes earlier," Seth replied as he shrugged his shoulders.

Rekler stood to the side of the door and pointed at it.

"Can you knock this down? We need to get out of here and find Oxford`."

Seth nodded his head and saw the door had buttons similar to the ones he had been fiddling with on the table cube earlier. He pressed one button after another until the door abruptly slid upwards so fast Seth jumped back in fright, hands ready to cause some damage.

"I could have knocked it down though," Seth said as he turned to Rekler with a smug grin on his face. Rekler laughed and they both walked through the doorway cautiously. The door led to a square room two metres deep, the walls of the room of which were a flawless shiny metal. Seth could see himself reflected almost perfectly: he had not managed to dodge much of the gore from the violent scene in the previous room.

The ceiling in the small room was a dark carpet-like texture, with a square, black metal panel in the centre. When Seth turned around to exit, he noticed next to the door were more small glowing buttons. They were all the same size — small green circles about three centimetres in diameter in two columns of ten. Seth pressed one at the top and the door flew shut with a loud clang.

Rekler looked at Seth; they were clearly both experiencing the same heavy, nauseous feeling. It quickly subsided and the door opened again. Now they were looking into a completely different room. It had the same motif as the last room, with many straight glowing green lines creeping across the walls, floor and ceiling, but the room was empty. Seth tried pressing another button and the door shut again. This time he felt lighter and not quite as nauseous, until the sensation disappeared entirely. The door opened once again, revealing yet another strange room filled with glowing green lines.

Rekler and Seth explored the building in this strange contraption, not meeting any other Inquirers as they did so. After ten different rooms, they emerged in a room with one wall coated in illuminated images. They both wanted to explore it a little: the images were all moving, showing real time feeds of different parts of Chos Garren. Rekler seemed to have a vague idea of what he was doing, as he immediately started pressing different buttons next to the small displays. The air filled with the strangest noise. To Seth it sounded like someone had picked up a guitar, detuned it beyond recognition and then began plucking the strings with their teeth; oddly enough, they were doing it in time with some unheard beat, so although it lacked harmony it did have rhythm.
Rekler turned to Seth with tears in his eyes, Seth was surprised by such a display of emotion from the tough man. Rekler gritted his teeth and smashed his hand down on the keyboard.

"This is where they control the clase! This is..." Rekler choked on his last words as emotion got the better of him. Rekler pressed the button that had activated the noise and it became silent except for a low humming in the room. Seth was puzzled: that noise was supposed to be the clase, but it just sounded like chaos. Exactly how could such a noise bring people to tears? Or a better question, make them happy? It had brought a tough guy like Rekler to tears so it was clearly pretty powerful stuff, but Seth had not been affected by it.

"Was that Chos Garren...onian music?" Seth asked Rekler.
Rekler wiped some tears from his face and responded his breathing now under control

"What? No, what is that? That was the clase. We have to stop it!"

"Well, this seems like a good place to do so. Wait, was that "ding" noise I kept hearing clase?" Seth asked Rekler hoping this would finally reveal the source. Rekler shrugged his shoulders in reply.

"Maybe? They play corrections through the speakers somejits to rebalance the harmony or modify the clase"

"The harmony? So it *is* music — but why's it so terrible?" Seth asked Rekler, no modicum of sarcasm behind his voice. Rekler looked surprised.

"Because they use this to control what people are feeling, they are no longer able to feel their – "

"No no, I mean why does it sound so terrible? 'Harmony' is probably the last word I would use to describe the sound I just heard." Seth noticed Rekler appeared to get a little offended as he heard Seth's description of clase.

"It *is* harmonious, Seth. Clase was once used for recreation, but when the Inquirers devised an equation linking clase directly to emotions, they turned it into something else. Look, this really isn't the time for this. I think I know how to shut this down. One of Katarina's blueprints taught us about this kind of machine. You go and find Oxford; I'm sure you can hold your own if you encounter any more Inquirers"

Seth agreed and reentered the strange room that moved him through the building by methods unknown. He faced the small panel of glowing buttons and pressed one that he hadn't tried yet. He had been going down the buttons one by one starting from the left column and noticed he was now feeling lighter between each room. Three rooms after Seth had left Rekler, he discovered a room containing a sight that would be seared into his memory: Oxford's lifeless body was lying on the floor, staring up at the ceiling, thrown on top of several other corpses. The walls in this room had far fewer glowing lines travailing its surface, so illumination was poor, amplifying the haunting atmosphere of the scene in front of Seth.

Seth could see about forty corpses scattered through the room. Very few of the resistance members now lying dead had any of the original white of their clothing still showing; their uniforms were now completely bloodied. The troopers had no wounds of any kind on their bodies, but their faces showed they had lost all their blood orally. Dried blood coated their necks and chins, but not the rest of their faces. Many bodies were just silhouettes, interrupting the few illuminating green lines in the walls. Seth had seen enough and pressed another button on the small panel to advance to the next room. Anywhere — he just needed to get away from this one filled with death.

The door opened up to one of the rooms he had already visited. It had a small table in the centre with a couple of gadgets. The lights travelling through the grooves in the walls and ceiling were coloured white in this chamber. Seth supported himself with both hands on the table and breathed deeply; he felt like throwing up. All of these people he had just met and started to respect — now dead. He had never had to witness so much death so close before. He could still see some faces with their eyes hanging open, staring into nothing. What kind of people were the Inquirers, to dismiss so many lives so easily? Had Seth and Rekler been the last two survivors, intended for the same fate? Everything started to blur. Seth looked around for some place he could get fresh air. He needed to get out of this building. With his retrieved jewellery that would be no problem.

Several thick shafts of steel shot from Seth's hands and created a huge dent in the wall opposite him. Seth continued to fire poles of metal, making their ends ever sharper, and suddenly a yellow light shone through a hole he had made in the wall. He fired several more humongous spikes and ran up to the resulting breach, poking his head through to look outside. Seth was inside the other Reference Centre tower; he could see the one he had assaulted alongside the resistance standing alone inside its smooth coating. He looked down, jumped out of the hole and summoned his trusty water propeller to lower himself safely to the ground. When he landed, Seth began to breathe normally again, the fresh air helping him regain his balance.

Seth had had enough of Chos Garren. He did want to help the resistance, but *his* goal was to get home. This really was not his fight, and it seemed like a fight he could not win either. Maybe Rekler would be able to shut down the clase, but eventually the other Inquirers would come and strangle him to death, like the rest of the resistance. Even if Seth were to help, the Inquirers would use their sonic blast again (or who knows what other powers they might have that Seth would not be prepared for). He did not feel like waking up to listen to another Inquirer ranting about the universe for an hour — nor did he want to end up a corpse.

The propeller made its familiar buzzing sound as Seth used it to lift himself into the air. When he was a kilometre above Estever's surface, he focused on his ring holding the small sample of molten metal inside a glass bead. The landscape beneath Seth got smaller and smaller as he grew bigger and bigger.

Chapter 9

The water propeller kept buzzing beneath Seth as he rose further and further above the surface of Estever. The towers he had assaulted with a team of fifty men were now just a small speck. Seth continued to ascend, trying to avoid becoming too huge too quickly in case he killed everyone in Chos Garren under his gargantuan sandal. The rim of Estever became visible and the familiar turquoise of the massive blue orbs was revealed. Seth felt a strange sensation as his head hit the frictionless surface of the atom, and the rest of his body fell on to the blue surface. He stood quickly, remembering there was no air in this part of his universe. He increased his size faster to climb back up to the surface of the atoms he had fallen in between.

One huge breath was left inside Seth's lungs, slowly turning to carbon dioxide as he desperately tried to escape his miniscule prison. The elemental that Seth had just been inhabiting continued along it's circuit of the atom. Soon it became so small Seth couldn't see it anymore; only the surface of the atom was visible now, and the many more above him. Once Seth was tall enough, he clamped one hand around a blue orb and tried to pull himself up. He couldn't help noticing he had lost a little muscle mass now that he had been manipulating matter as transport instead of the old-fashioned pedestrian method. Running out of air was now a distinct possibility, so Seth accelerated his growth even further and flew upwards, bumping into atoms on the way — and possibly knocking thousands of civilisations into their own version of The Abyss.

Suffocating was a terrible feeling. Seth's lungs felt like they were on fire as he continued on his flight. He wanted to cough so badly but he knew that that would certainly end it all. Suddenly there were far fewer turquoise orbs floating in the air in front of Seth; he could still see a few, but nothing like the mess that had just played pinball with his body. He was almost completely out of breath and in his panic to find some oxygen, he grew a little *too* quickly. Both of Seth's feet were now too big to fit on his segment. He waved his hands around as he attempted to balance himself, slowly shrinking until he was the right size — he hoped. He didn't have any reference point for his original size; he had not planned for the eventuality of his massive size fluctuation.

The vegetable garden didn't seem to have suffered terribly in his absence. In actuality, he had only been gone two of his nights, though it felt a lot longer. So much had happened during his short time on Estever — a planet that Seth had probably just kicked into oblivion. He thought back to his journey between the 'atoms' that apparently were the particles making up his universe. He had bounced around so much and grown so big he had no idea how much damage he could have caused. He started to think about it: right now, was he crushing *trillions* of elementals just by standing still? If so, he had already killed an inconceivable amount in his lifetime. He could not make much of a difference in the grand scheme of things... he couldn't live his life thinking about how he was murdering entire civilisations everywhere he went. Even the air was made of these particles; they were probably smashing into him with the wind.

Seth had seen enough death, and from extremely close range. He didn't want to cause any more. He began to think about how he had left Rekler down there, in the grass, on one of its atoms. That scene was not something he would easily forget, no matter how much he wanted to. He thought about how it wasn't entirely noble of him to leave the way he did.

But to be fair, I kind of panicked after seeing about fifty dead bodies strangled to death and dumped like ragdolls.

Even if he wanted to go back to help Rekler shut down the clase, it would be impossible to find the exact atom he was on again, never mind the elemental on that atom. The world was much more complicated than he had realised, and probably more than he could *ever* realise. Not long ago Seth was living in a world that only contained three thousand people, shrouded in a white mist. He had never even dreamed there was a whole world beneath his, and that this world would be made from other worlds inhabited by beings made of other worlds. Seth's head spun from the complexity of the puzzle he was trying to assemble in his mind. He might need to draw this one day to try to understand it; for now he would get some food into him.

Seth sighed in relief when his matter manipulation convinced his passionfruit vine to grow several more burgeoning tendrils. Purple fruits hung from small stems, causing the vine to sag with their weight. Seth plucked three and smiled in relief, enjoying the knowledge that he could once again draw on any kind of matter in his surroundings for his powers. Seth walked inside his small cottage and cut open the purple fruits on a plate so he could feast on the yellow-black seeds inside. As Seth happily crunched his food, sitting back home at last, he began to think about his next plan. Maybe he could try searching for Swevender again —although he had only been gone two days and his skills hadn't really improved *that* much. Yes, though necessity had driven him to push the limits of his abilities and he had definitely learned a few things, but he didn't want to encounter anyone with abilities like the Inquirers again, nor anyone as cold-blooded.
The best course of action Seth could think of was that he should just keep exploring the landscape around him. He still had some small hope that something had survived the shockwave that had destroyed the world's surface. While he was journeying above the surface of the planet, he could try to hone his abilities by practising techniques Red had taught him. Soon enough Seth would be able to elevate his small concrete vessel to the same altitude as Swevender and then he could truly begin his search.

FALLEN WORLD

***

A week later, Seth finally had a normal night's sleep. He had managed to keep himself distracted for long enough so that visions of lifeless bodies sprawled across a poorly lit room didn't haunt him, and he drifted into a deep slumber. That day he also found a strange statue in the middle of the barren landscape beneath his floating concrete ship. He had travelled to the surface to investigate it. Once again it was a statue of two people, a woman and a man. These two, however, did not entirely resemble the statue he had seen in the Restyard, though it seemed to be carved from the same, unusual stone. The woman was much shorter, with hair stopping just above her shoulders. She was also wearing a different kind of cloak with a lot more patterns decorating it. Part of the woman's face had crumbled away, making it impossible to see possible facial similarities. The man had a long, pointed chin and deep sunken eyes, also wearing a long cloak, but his statue seemed completely untouched. It left Seth thinking more about the recurring appearance of two wizards in his travels. Such thoughts were a welcome distraction from his most recent experience in Chos Garren.

When he woke up, his first thought was that he had finally been able to sleep normally — which reminded him why that was remarkable, which brought up more flashbacks. But he was getting better. He had been able to eat well, since he could manipulate any bit of matter and food would appear, begging him to eat it. He usually thought back to the steak Katja had cooked when he was in Chos Garren; that was the best meal he had had recently. His food manipulation skills were getting better, and the fruit and vegetables were of an even better quality than when Swevender was still agglomerated.

Today was rather warm, with the sun shining strong. There were very few clouds and just a slight breeze, bringing with it the same dusty smell it always had nowadays. He scanned the landscape beneath his segment: flat, brown and featureless as usual. The wind started to pick up unexpectedly and travelled in a circle beneath Seth's home. The spinning air darkened and a miniature tornado appeared, smashing the earthen column that had held Seth above the ground while he slept on his concrete ship. The segment shook violently as Seth struggled to control the swirling mass of wind beneath him. He descended quickly, floating for a few seconds as the downward acceleration of his segment exceeded that of gravity. His body thumped down against the grass as his vessel slowed its descent. Eventually everything felt stable again and Seth was once more flying confidently on his little piece of Swevender. It was not long before he finally saw something in the distance: it looked like a small network of villages, but Seth needed to be closer to get a better idea. He manifested his waterscope and peered towards the objects in the distance.

It looked like a bunch of dirt piles, but on some of the small hills Seth could see what looked like doors, or windows, and there appeared to be paths between the small mounds. In fact, if Seth pretended the hills were all houses, then it looked like a perfectly normal village. There were several farms which were apparently able to protect their crops from the shockwave, the fields still filled with green grass and orange trees, surrounded by wooden fences. Other fields held different kinds of fruit and plants, and long yellow grass filled many of the paddocks. There were also some cows in one of the fields, but compared to the houses they looked enormous. One cow could easily have trampled the entire village back into dust, but the fence around the livestock was appropriately sized to prevent them from doing so.

Now that Seth was getting closer he noticed the same could be said of the trees growing in the outer paddocks. If he was estimating correctly, the hill-houses were only one metre high. There was some movement other than the giant cows visible now: moving along the paths between the small hovels were the villagers. They were definitely not human, but looked small and alien to Seth. A small, wide ball comprised the body and face of the strange creature, and it had one leg elevating the body about thirty centimetres from the ground. The face of the creature, however, had an oddly human look. Sticking from the side of the body was one arm, almost always grasping a strange looking staff. The creatures moved along quite nimbly, using the staff as a second leg. The tip of each staff seemed to have some sort of claw — some of them even had a metal hand on the end of their staffs.

Seth wanted to investigate a little more before he lowered his segment to the ground. He floated over the farming areas towards the centre of the small village. Some of the hills here were multi-tiered with a much higher concentration of creatures hopping about. Through the waterscope Seth studied the villagers. There were a few houses made of wood, but mainly on the farms; inside the city, dirt seemed to be the favourite construction material. It was quite a bland looking town overall, with hardly any plant life to break up the monotony of brown.

The creatures coming in and out of the small homesteads had skin of pale grey, with a slight green tint; it was a colour that didn't improve the aesthetics of the village. A few fences of a light brown wood were scattered through the town. Some seemed to be protecting invisible gardens while others just surrounded areas with no visible reason to justify a fence being there in the first place. Seth decided he would dock his small vessel just outside the village. He directed his segment in a straight line towards the rural areas again, then slowly descended to the ground. Seth summoned a small dirt cradle to hold his segment straight: he wanted to avoid having everything in his house roll to one corner again. He lowered himself slowly from the segment, manipulating the air around him and blowing a lot of the dust up into the air. He dusted off his robe off and started walking towards the village.

Seth soon came across one of the locals, and it stopped to inspect him. This creature had its arm sticking out from its right side and the tip of its staff had a device with eight blades in two rows of four sticking from the top. The blades had a worn looking black holster covering their pointed ends, and looked like the two rows of metal teeth could be used to pick up small objects. The creature inspected Seth.

"Greetings traveller! I didn't realise anyone had survived the shockwave. Welcome to Dewall, a home of the Evodents! It is a relief to know that at least some humans survived. Are there any others with you?"

Seth did not expect to hear the creature talking Common and was caught off guard slightly. He stared a few seconds before he answered.

"Uhh, no, nobody else with me... how did *you* survive the shockwave?"

The creature laughed softly.

"We are protected by a barrier, created by two very smart people — but someone with more knowledge can tell you more about that. I have to tend to my crops, but do you need directions?" he asked Seth.

"Yes, where is the centre of Dewall from here?" Seth asked the Evodent. He had seen the village clearly when he was floating, but on the ground Seth's sense of direction was still terrible. The creature frowned.

"Don't know why you would want to go there boy, too many people, too busy. But if you really need to go, it's that way." The creature used his staff to indicate that Seth should continue on the same heading. Seth bent his body forward slightly, bowing in thanks to the farmer, and continued towards the centre of Dewall. Seth could hear shouting in the distance as he passed more fields lined with rows of trees.

The cow's mooing became softer as Seth approached the centre of the village. Many of the creatures stopped in their tracks to stare at Seth, while others kept walking while obviously looking at him. Seth knew from his encounter with the little farmer that this town was no stranger to humans but it also seemed he was the first one they had seen since the shockwave a month ago.

Seth really had no idea where to go, but the fact that this town had survived meant it must to have had some sort of defensive technology — or the inhabitants were also capable of matter manipulation. In the Restyard, Red had told Seth that it was more than likely that anything capable of surviving the shockwave was probably a creation of the element binders Jacobus or Iselle. If they were here in Dewall at one point, it was very possible some highly valuable knowledge had been left behind, something that might help Seth control his matter manipulation enough to elevate his segment back to Swevender's altitude. He decided to explore the village a bit more to acquaint himself with the layout; maybe then there would be some indication as to where he could look or who he could ask.

From ground level the village revealed as little about itself as it did from Seth's previous vantage point. The hills were definitely houses; their petiteness was explained by the size of the creatures inhabiting them. Seth very much doubted he could fit inside any of them. Towards the centre, however, there seemed to be much bigger dirt structures. Their doors were still only high enough to let the Evodents through, but Seth thought if he really wanted to, he could crawl his way in. Still feeling conscious of the villagers watching him, Seth paused to look around. He heard more

shouting in the distance and a few of the creatures hopping around stopped to look towards the noise. Seth headed towards the source of the shouting; over the tops of the buildings he could see a lot of the Evodents' staffs, all congregated in one area.
Around some corners and past more dirt huts, Seth saw ten of the creatures talking amongst each other. They suddenly stopped as Seth came into view, and two of the creatures approached Seth.

"Hello human. We heard you just arrived?" asked one of the Evodents. Its staff jingled as it moved its arm slightly; it had a variety of metal devices hanging from it on small hooks. Seth was surprised word about his arrival already seemed to be common knowledge despite arriving less than thirty minutes ago.

"Yes, I was passing by and I was curious how such a village could have survived the shockwave so I –" Seth was interrupted before he could begin introducing himself.

"Yes yes, we have a barrier, but when did you arrive? There seems to have been some trouble on the outskirts of Dewall," said the second creature, whose staff seemed much simpler than the rest of his companions. The creature was speaking rather aggressively and Seth didn't like the implication that he was responsible for whatever the trouble was.
Seth knew he hadn't done anything wrong, so he decided honesty would be the best approach;

"I got here about twenty minutes ago and I haven't done anything since I got here. I did meet a farmer who told me this was Dewall, home of the Evodents — but I had never heard of them before."
The other creature's staff jingled as he took a hop closer to Seth with an irritated look on its face.

"We are Evodents. I am an Evodent. Both of us are Evodents! Where have you been boy? Humans and Evodents have known about each other since I was born!"
The other Evodent spoke now:

"Yes, I find it quite surprising that you don't know about us. You came here twenty minutes ago you say… well, we have a few more questions for you. Would you accompany us please?" The Evodent signalled to his colleague holding the staff with hanging metal objects, whose staff jingled as he hopped behind Seth and proceeded to nudge him forward.

The Evodent that had spoken last looked at Seth and then led the way, hopping down a path between some dirt huts. Seth was curious as to what was about to happen; maybe he had inadvertently broken some law by arriving here. He was quite sure he hadn't done anything wrong so he decided he would cooperate. And it seemed the Evodent's request was not something Seth should say no to, so he gracefully acquiesced. The Evodent behind him started pushing a little harder and pointed parts of his staff actually hurt a little. Seth turned around.

"Ow! Take it easy! I am cooperating!"

The creature, who already looked angry, seemed to get even angrier at Seth's exclamation and took in a deep breath to respond, but he was interrupted by the other Evodent.

"Nigel, just walk behind him. We don't even know if the human did it." The creature, Nigel, ceased poking Seth's back, and they continued their walk through the village in silence.

The three stopped at the front of a dirt building much larger than the rest, with a relatively huge door.

"Since you are new to Dewall, I should explain that humans do not have the best reputation here. In fact, they are renowned for being underhanded scoundrels, and we have rarely been proved wrong. Your race is the reason our incarceration centre is the biggest building in Dewall," said the more reasonable Evodent to Seth. He opened the door and signalled Seth to walk through first, closely followed by Nigel.

Chapter 10

The Evodents were a strange sort of creature. The tallest one only came up to Seth's knee. They were so small it seemed impossible they had enough room for a digestive system, never mind a brain large enough to support sentient behaviour. Seth had seen some strange things from his year in the Restyard but interacting with it directly felt much more confronting; a ball about forty centimetres wide with human facial features stood on its one leg explaining to Seth why he had been brought to the incarceration centre.

"Sorry about my colleague Nigel. He's a unipedalist, always gets a bit nervous around creatures with more than one leg," said the Evodent that had led them inside. "My name is Gary, you can sit on the floor over there," Gary told Seth, gesturing to the opposite side of the room they had just entered.

The incarceration centre had unusual architecture: the roof was higher than necessary while the floor space was extremely limited. There was a path recessed into the wall, tracing a spiral route around the circumference of the room. It sloped upwards, and looked like it was used by the Evodents as stairs. The inside of the room was the same light brown colour that all the domiciles in Dewall seemed to be made from; so was the furniture, of which there was very little. A small staircase leading to a seat facing a large table in the centre of the room. Gary was hopping up the staircase, assisting his bouncing with his simple silver and black staff. There was no longer any sign of Nigel. Seth seated himself on the floor and leaned against the wall. Strange that they made the building to accommodate humans but they hadn't made any human sized furniture beyond a huge table currently being used by a hopping ball that came up to Seth's knee.

Only the tip of Gary's head poking up from behind the table was visible from where Seth was sitting. Seth saw some papers being tapped against the table and small thuds as Gary opened up drawers in the side of the table, making a low grinding noise as the furniture seemed to made from dried mud. Gary leapt onto the surface of the table so he could look properly at Seth sitting on the floor.

"So you saw a farmer did you? It just so happens that this incident occurred out in one of the rural districts. Was the farmer's name Michael?" Gary asked Seth as he hopped back and forth on the surface of the table.

Seth still had no idea what was going on but he continued to cooperate. Despite his ability to easily escape this situation, he knew keeping his patience was the quickest route to illumination.

"I don't know the farmer's name, I just asked him for directions to the centre of Dewall and the next... uh, person I interacted with was you."

Gary stopped his bouncing and pirouetted to face Seth. He stared in silence for a few seconds before he responded.

"Well, what did he look like?"

Seth looked at the ceiling as he tried to recall any distinctive features of the farmer.

"Well, he looked like you: a ball with one leg and one arm, only his staff thing looked like it had some kind of bread slicer on it."

"Yes yes, very funny boy, we all look the same to you humans don't we? You lot are so obnoxious. I will only tolerate your rudeness for so long, this is a serious matter!" Gary's volume increased throughout the sentence until he was almost shouting.

"Well I don't want to be rude. What exactly is the serious matter you're talking about?"

Gary's eyes widened and he began his response with a hoarse cough.

"Hurumph. The serious matter is that one of our citizens has been killed — cut entirely in half, very strange phenomenon, and I can't even imagine any Evodents having the means to commit such a gruesome crime. Then you show up at exactly the same time. Wouldn't you call that suspicious?"

"Woah! Cut in half? Are you serious? Well it wasn't me! I only came here to get information; I wanted to know more about your town's barrier. Killing someone is not any part of my quest, and certainly doesn't help me reach the goal of said quest," Seth said to Gary. In lieu of an eyebrow, the ridge above one of Gary's eyes rose and he looked skeptically at Seth.

"All the humans I have met know about the barrier, and they also know not to cause trouble here. They know we have the means to disable you humans, and cells big enough to keep you in while you think about your misdeeds. So how about you start telling the truth, you pink, fleshy biped!" Gary jumped down from the table and hopped rapidly towards Seth.

Gary whacked Seth on the head with the end of his staff, making clear to Seth why he was instructed to sit on the floor. He grabbed the staff and attempted to wrench it from Gary's grasp, but Gary refused to let go and was launched into the air along with his staff. Gary adeptly spun around the pole on his one hand, and his foot connected painfully with Seth's jaw. Seth threw the staff away from him with Gary still holding it. Gary stabbed the staff into the ground and did a skilful back flip as he was flying through the air, landing safely on his single foot. He held the staff horizontally above his head and began spinning it threateningly. Nigel came bursting through a door, waving his staff around violently, screaming

"Taste metal you bipedal freak!"

Seth stood up as Nigel hopped towards him. He did not want to hurt the Evodent but he didn't feel like another whack from one of their staffs either. Seth raised his palm towards the aggressive little sphere bouncing toward him, and the dry mud of the floor extended to form a small cage around the little creature.

"What?! What is this?" Nigel began asking himself out loud.

Gary looked at Seth with a look of shock on his face.

"H-h-how did you do that?"

Seth smiled as he responded.

"I am a manipulator of matter, and contrary to what you think, you do not have the means to throw me in any cell. But I did *not* cut anyone in half, that really doesn't help me, or anyone. Do you believe me?"

Nigel superfluously threw his staff in Seth's direction, falling well short of causing any harm with a metallic thud.

"Don't listen to him boss! That two-footed freak will make a pillow out of your remains!"

Gary ignored the screaming Nigel and hopped slowly in Seth's direction. Seth raised his hand the same way he had when he imprisoned Nigel. The Evodent froze, pushing the black end of his staff against the ground. Seth hoped he could explain to the two Evodents that their efforts were in vain, and he needed their help. He would clearly have to prove his innocence before they would divulge anything useful. Seth broke the silence.

"So, despite what Nigel may say, I'm not actually here to cause any trouble, nor did I. I only wanted to ask you for help, but I have the idea that won't come easily"

Gary stared at Seth, his arm was still holding the staff tensely with an impressively small amount of movement.

"So, how about I find out who killed the farmer? I can be very persuasive and resourceful. I get you some answers, and you give some to me?" Seth asked the static Gary over Nigel's scornful laughter from his mud prison.

About thirty seconds of silence passed and Seth was about to open his mouth to try again, but Gary spoke a split second earlier.

"How do I know you won't just run away?"

"Well, I could just do that — to be honest you really couldn't stop me." Seth clicked his fingers and a stream of sparks jetted upwards from the palm of his hand as he continued talking.

"The fact that I am still here is a sign that I am cooperating. I know the evidence points towards me being the culprit, but I think your prejudice for humans is also playing a part here. I think I can show you just how honest we can actually be."

Gary's eyes fixated on the stream of sparks fountaining from Seth's hand as he responded.

"Yes, well, I guess there is always an exception… how do you plan on finding the culprit?"

Seth smiled; he was getting somewhere with this Evodent. He let the streams of sparks dissipate.

"Well you will need to tell me what you know so far, and I will need some sort of verhil, uh, map, so I can find my way around."

Gary's arm loosened its grip on the metal staff as he began talking calmly with Seth, about the town of Dewall and the recent murder. Seth still hadn't mastered the art of making matter disappear, so he made himself a jagged metal staff and carefully broke the mud bars encasing Nigel. Nigel hopped back towards the door, muttering curses about bipeds. Seth sat cross-legged on the floor while Gary explained the situation to Seth from atop his mud table.

An hour later Seth was walking towards the south of Dewall in search of an Evodent called Lauren. She was the one that had found the victim lying in two halves. The victim's name was Chris and he was – according to Gary – a very peaceful person. He lived alone on his farm. Sometimes he had people to help him, when tending the farm alone became too much at the turn of a good season, but otherwise not many people saw him.

FALLEN WORLD

Dewall was actually one of many small towns housing the Evodents; there were two neighbouring villages to the north of Dewall, both much larger. These villages were called Jesterton and Lurless. Dewall was the southernmost village of a larger network, and was mainly a farming town.

According to the map Seth had borrowed from Gary he was getting close to Lauren's property. He looked up from his map and on the side of the path was a gate in the fence bordering the road. Seth approached the gate and peered over it: in the distance across a green grass field he saw a small mud house. He opened the gate and walked across the field slowly. Around him he heard the mooing of cows. He suddenly realised the fence of this property actually came up to his chest; it hadn't registered before because to Seth that was the size it *should* have been. The fences of this property were clearly built to keep cows and not like the knee-high fences he had been seeing on the way to Lauren's cow farm. As he got closer to the cottage, Seth saw some cows moving around just beyond the small abode.

Two hundred metres further and Seth knelt down so he could knock on the door of the small mud hut. But just before his hand made contact with the door, Seth saw something strange: one of the cows had started running as if something were chasing it. Seth noticed that its udder was much larger than the rest of the cows', almost double in size. As the animal was running, what looked like a piece of its udder fell to the ground and stood up on one leg. This must have been Lauren; apparently she was the cause of the cow's distress. It stopped running once she had let go of its udder.

Seth approached her. The small Evodent had one left arm, holding a coil of rope with an end knotted around her ankle. She still hadn't noticed Seth and continued her activity. The arm holding the rope threw it lasso-style and caught the udder of the now-still cow, then pulled back quickly on the rope to tighten the end encircling the cow's udder. The cow mooed in distress and starting running as it had earlier. The Evodent pulled herself along the rope while being dragged, grasping the rope between her teeth and then her hand. Eventually she was back with one foot on the udder, standing horizontally with the rope between her teeth. She wrapped her leg with more rope to secure herself and then used her free hand to grab a small glass container held against her body with a length of rope. She put the bottle between her teeth and her body tipped upside down until the glass bottle was directly under one of the teats. The Evodent then proceeded to squeeze milk from the udder with her hand, catching it in the bottle. She continued until the glass container was almost full.

The cow was still running but it had slowed down, either from fatigue or resignation. Eventually it stopped and the Evodent dropped off. She now had the glass bottle in her hand and was tumbling through the grass, not spilling a single drop. She jumped up and hopped to a table nearby where many full bottles of milk stood. As the female Evodent placed the bottle on the table she looked up and saw Seth watching her. She used her one arm to swing the rope so it coiled around her shoulder, and hopped towards Seth.

"Well, I didn't know any humans had managed to survive the shockwave! What are you doing on my property?" The small creature bouncing towards Seth had a very smooth voice that sounded like it came solely from the back of the throat. He imagined she would have a great singing voice.

"My apologies, I came here on behalf of Gary, the... chief of police, I guess? I wanted to ask you about the body you found," Seth said to the female Evodent.

"Ah, ok. I would have appreciated Gary being here too — it's not often you find a human investigating a murder in Dewall."

"You are Lauren, right?" Seth asked the tiny lady.

She looked at Seth without the slightest sign of emotion.

"Yes."

"And you believe the death of Chris was a murder?" Seth asked as a cow mooed in the background.

Lauren looked up at Seth and took a hop backwards as she spoke.

"Yes of course! The poor man was cut in half, nothing natural about that! And he never hurt anyone I tell you. We would say hello to each other every day at midday over the fence, without fail, but today I looked over the fence and didn't see him anywhere."

Seth looked at Lauren thoughtfully not saying anything, so she continued with her story.

"I called out his name but heard nothing. I wanted to find him so we could have one of our chats, but found his body cut in half with bloody grass all around him! The halves were cut so perfectly it *couldn't* be a natural phenomenon. To be honest, it's something I would expect from a human. Did you bring anyone with you when you came here?"

Again Seth stood in silence looking down at Lauren. He exhaled deeply.

"No, I came here alone. I don't know why humans have such a bad reputation here; where I come from they are honest, caring people... well, mostly... well, actually no they're not, especially stupid Kurt." Seth stood looking at the Evodent, she seemed to be backing away slowly but with one foot it was difficult to make it look subtle. Seth continued.

"Okay. I see why humans might have a bad reputation, we are not *all* nice people, but surely you have the same among your Evodents right? I mean, what were you doing to that poor cow when I arrived here? That didn't look very pleasant." Lauren stopped shuffling backwards through the grass and looked at the cow.

"I was milking her! She was a little bit spooked today so she's not cooperating — that's why I had to get the milking rope out — but I treat Artemisia and all the other cows just fine," and a cow mooed as if to agree with her.

Seth looked at the cow which had now turned to stare at him and Lauren. Its tail appeared intermittently as it swung back and forth, catching Seth's eye. He noticed the small tuft of hair that normally tipped a cow's tail was trimmed in a very neat straight line.

"And you shave all of their tails too?" Seth asked, gesturing towards poor, spooked Artemisia. The look on Lauren's face changed to one of surprise and she turned around to look at said cow.

"What?" she said as she hopped to Artemisia to inspect her tail. "Well, I believe you found the reason she was spooked, Mr. Human — probably the same thing that killed Chris."

Seth raised one eyebrow as he looked at the tail of the cow and back to Lauren.

"Hmm, maybe, but I prefer to collect more evidence before I start coming to those kinds of conclusions."

Lauren looked at Seth as she spoke "That is wise, but he didn't just cut Artemisia's tail, he cut all the branches from one side of the oak tree on Chris' property too. And cut one of the trees on my property in half too, as well as slicing up poor Chris during his journey."

Seth brought his hand up to his chin as he thought about what Lauren had just said. Apparently some force had cut a straight line, beginning from the oak tree in the distance to this tree that Lauren had just pointed out. The tree on Laurens property had a perfect slice through the middle of the trunk. Both halves were leaning slightly away from each other, no longer clinging together, and would probably fall over in time. Whatever had cut the tree had almost certainly sliced Chris in half, and Artemisia's tail hairs right off.

Seth finished his train of thought and stopped staring at the sky to look back at Lauren but she spoke before he could ask anything.

"The only thing I can think of is either one of those cursed humans — sorry — did it, or they have made some sort of new technology in Stique that hasn't reached Dewall yet."

Seth closed his mouth, forgetting what he was going to ask Lauren. He was honestly not the best investigator, but he wanted to show these people that humans deserved a better reputation — maybe not the *best* reputation but certainly they were not the first people to think of when mentioning criminals or rapscallions. Seth formulated a new question.

"How do I get to Stique? I think I want to ask some questions there."

Lauren suddenly became friendly, although most likely it was because she realised he was about to leave and she could get on with her bovine acrobatics. She led Seth into her small cottage and showed him a map displaying the network of all the villages of the Evodents. Stique was about three villages above Dewall. It was the centre of all of the villages and seemed to have the most complex network of roads. Seth put his hand to the map and an exact replica appeared in the air next to it. It drifted to the ground, causing Lauren to jump. He picked up his copy of the map and left the house as he said goodbye to her. Seth thought she had a rather strange look on her face as he left — but all Evodent faces looked strange to him. Hunger inspired him to head back to his home and grab something from his garden.

Seth propelled himself through the sky, manipulating the air currents beneath him and noticed he was improving and even getting more stylish at it. Once he was high enough, he spotted his house just outside one of the nearby farms. There were five Evodents gathered around it. Seth flung himself towards the segment, still saddled in dirt, and eased himself down onto the grass. The Evodents around him shouted with surprise as he landed. They had been attempting to climb their way onto his segment. The Evodents scattered like frightened rodents before Seth had time to respond.

Seth lifted his concrete ship into the air with his usual snaking tunnel of fierce wind. When he looked down at the ground it seemed completely peaceful, with only the air directly beneath him moving. He grabbed a handful of vegetables from his garden and began munching on them. He then looked at the map he had reproduced, and directed his vessel towards Stique, the largest city of Evodents.

It only took about thirty minutes for Seth to reach the outskirts of Stique. The towns might have been big by Evodent standards, but for Seth and his flying house it had been a minor journey; he had actually gone quite slowly so he could comfortably finish eating his lunch. Seth parked his house in a cradle of dirt again, but this time about fifty metres above ground level to avoid any Evodent incursions into his house. Then he eased himself to the ground to begin exploring the town of Stique. The houses here were bigger and had many more doors and windows. There were Evodents everywhere, none of whom had the time to stop and stare at Seth. A lot of them here were carrying the same type of staff, the top of which was an almost exact replica of a hand, only the surface was unnaturally smooth and it appeared to have two opposable thumbs.

Seth tried his hardest to avoid stepping on any Evodents as he explored Stique, but his concern was unnecessary, as they seemed to scatter before him; like a shark through a school of fish. Apparently the Evodents here were used to humans. Seth noticed some of the buildings were actually taller than him, and seemed like they would be very complicated inside. There were many balconies and staircases encompassing the outside of the buildings. The dirt here seemed to be darker and of a higher quality; most of the buildings actually had what could be called

FALLEN WORLD

corners, unlike Dewall's rounded piles of dirt. Seth came to an open plane with a few trees scattered about. Many Evodents were lying in the grass surrounding the trees, some in groups chatting while others were sitting alone performing various activities.

Some of the Evodents here seemed to be doubled; it looked like some of them had actually been fused together, creating a creature with two legs and two arms. These coupled were the only Evodents who did not carry a staff. It seemed that with two legs the paired Evodents no longer had any need for a staff to stabilise them and could function as a biped. Seth imagined that Nigel would not be very impressed by Stique. Seth bent over to ask two paired Evodents walking past him now about their different appearance.

"Excuse me, may I ask you two something?" Seth asked, loud enough to get their attention.

A few people stopped to look at him. It almost seemed like they were laughing at Seth before they resumed relaxing in the park. The two joined Evodents stopped and looked at Seth, confused. They spoke to each other like Seth was not even there.

"Is he speaking to us? Hmm, he must not know" said the right Evodent in a deep voice.

"No, I don't think he does dear. We can't hear you human — do you see any ears here?" said the left Evodent in a feminine voice.

Seth looked up from the two and scanned his surroundings. The Evodents all had one ear on their bodies, and the ear was opposite whichever side their arm was on. He looked back at the couple and realised they were joined right where their ears would be, so apparently this pairing sacrificed the Evodents' hearing. It seemed a strange thing to do, only being able to communicate with one person for the rest of your life, but apparently the Evodents saw this melding as being worth the sacrifice. Seth apologised, but realising straight away they couldn't hear him, he bowed slightly. Seth was already bent over slightly so he was in danger of falling over and waved his arms around slightly as he regained his balance. The two Evodents eyes moved to look at each other, and then they walked away.

There weren't that many double Evodents walking around. Stique was still a hopping city for the most part, but there was always at least a couple within eyesight. On the other side of the park (which was actually quite large even for human standards — it seemed the Evodents took their recreation very seriously) there stood many Evodents close together. There were two groups standing in rows, all facing one Evodent who stood on a raised platform in front. Behind the Evodent on the platform were colourful fabrics fashioned into a small tent. The one-footed being was making a speech, so Seth moved in closer to hear what he was saying.

When Seth could hear him properly, it turned out to be a her, and she was talking about some kind of sacred union.

"... it is important that we leave these two with a good noise, a nice sound. They are not sacrificing their hearing, but focusing on each other. After the sacred melding they will be able to hear each other better than ever, and only each other. Many are too scared, too frightened to take such a leap like this, but Shaun and Linda have grown so close to each other they have decided to meld. When the barrier-builders created us so many years ago, they gave us the gift of love, and the love between these two is so deep they need only hear each other's voices for the rest of their lives."

Seth started listening extra intently now; the mention of "barrier-builders" had piqued his interest. He was still at a complete loss as to how this network of villages had survived the shockwave that tore Swevender apart. Seth felt like this moment could point him towards something or someone associated with matter manipulation, or element binding.

The Evodent continued her speech.

FALLEN WORLD

"Shaun and Linda are behind me while we perform the sacred melding. We are almost at the stage where they lose their ability to hear us; I would like you all to go into the tent, one by one, and say the last things you would like them to hear from you."

The Evodents all rose a few inches. Seth realised this was them standing up, and one of the melding participants hopped forward. The speaker pivoted to the side and held her hand out to welcome the Evodent as it disappeared inside the tent. One minute later the Evodent reappeared and hopped back to its original spot. The Evodent adjacent hopped forward and bounced into the tent, taking only thirty seconds to say their last message. There were tears running down its face as it moved back to its place. This went on until almost all of the Evodents had been in and out of the tent. The speaker shouted things every now and again: "Praise the builders of the barriers, the creator of the Evodents" and "Together, the Wandering Cross is only a short walk away".

Seth was curious as to what was going on inside the tent. He brought his hand up to focus on the small silver bead on the ring circling his middle finger. He became smaller and smaller, but at a much more controlled rate than he had the first time he tried. When he was about two centimetres tall, he started to fly through the middle of the proceedings and into the tent. Inside the tent lay two Evodents, ear to ear with their eyes rolling up into the back of their heads. Seth was a little shocked and stared at them. There was another Evodent standing next to the them. The two Evodents were lying on a metal table and there were short metal poles sticking out of the ground surrounding the table. The conscious Evodent supported himself with the poles, and moved around from pole to pole.

Seth was sent flying through the air as another Evodent pushed the tent flap open to enter. He steadied his floating; it seemed to be much easier than normal. Being so small made him much lighter and with less weight to blow around. Seth turned around and saw a fourth Evodent hopping towards the table. He stopped just short of the two Evodents, now almost drooling. His last words to them were trembling with emotion:

"You two have made me the saddest Evodent alive. I would have travelled to The Wandering Cross and back ten times for you Linda, I would have fought the Twins for you. I can't believe you would fall in love with an oaf like Shaun. I wanted to be an adult about this but I think the most adult thing is to be honest, no matter how much you don't want to hear it. But it's too late anyway, you and Shaun are here on the slab together and the Domestic just needs to perform the last few steps. I already hate the sound of Shaun's voice — I hope the same doesn't happen to you, Linda," and the sad Evodent hopped back outside, slumping his one shoulder.

Seth realised he was intruding on something a bit too personal and started to follow the melancholy homunculi outside, but he decided he wanted to see this melding process. A few more Evodents came in and said their last goodbyes, which were much sweeter than the first Seth had witnessed. Eventually he heard the hostess' voice again, although he was not quite sure it was her; the pitch of everything seemed to be lower at his current two centimetre tall size.

"Those were the last words Linda and Shaun will hear from you. I hope you all said what you needed to say," bellowed the hostess' voice into the tent.

The third Evodent circling Shaun and Linda on the table picked up a small container from the ground. It looked like a tiny sun inside a glass box. The Evodent balanced it so it lay on top of both Linda and Shaun. The Evodent pushed them against each other, then he raised his hand slowly towards the glass box, and flicked it. The box surrounding the small star shattered. The star itself made a small rumbling noise and a glowing plasma ring the same colour as the small yellow sun expanded outwards. The light was almost blinding and Seth had to look away for a few seconds. When he looked back he could just see the blue afterglow of the tiny supernova. Once the floating blue image died away, he saw the star was back inside its glass cube as if nothing had just happened. The conscious Evodent grabbed the glass cube and placed it on the ground behind him again, and Seth saw that the two Evodents were now joined at the ear, one being, no evidence of the two ever being separate. Seth was completely shocked: he had just witnessed some kind of matter manipulation, but clearly from an extremely skilled wielder.

A two centimetre tall Seth flew back to where he had shrunk himself. There were several puzzled-looking Evodents gathered around where he had been standing. Seth decided it would be best to return to his original size elsewhere. He glided through the air until he could barely see the confused Evodents scratching their heads with their staffs, searching for the human that was just here. Seth looked at the silver bead ring and began growing. When he was almost his original size, he realised he was actually standing next to the Evodents searching for him; apparently he hadn't quite grasped the scale difference when he shrank.
As Seth grew in size he realised that he wasn't so sure how big he should become. The Evodents were quite small to him but he was not familiar enough with their general breadth and height to be able to use them as a reference. He figured being slightly smaller might help in his quest — less intimidating. The Evodents might prove to be more cooperative.

Seth heard yelling. He thought his size manipulation trick might have frightened some Stique citizens but the yelling was coming from the distance. A group of Evodents carrying simple black and silver staffs were running swiftly towards Seth.

"There he is!" shouted the Evodent leading the pack, pointing towards Seth with his staff.

FALLEN WORLD

Chapter 11

Once again Seth found himself in a familiar setting: the inside of this incarceration centre was very similar to the one in Dewall, although clearly had seen a lot more use. The leader of the Stique police was hopping back and forth on the table and Seth had some sort of bindings holding his hands together. The metal of the bindings was extremely light but also very strong. He made a mental note to be sure to take a sample of it when he left here. The bindings had been applied by two separate Evodents before Seth could even react: they had slapped their staffs against his wrists and the metal coiled instantly around Seth's wrists, threading itself through the other staff's hoop and stiffening to make an incredibly restricting knot. Seth was now sitting on the floor, alone with one other Evodent. Apparently word about Seth had not quite travelled from Dewall yet, or they surely would have posted more guards... this Evodent officer was most likely quite agile, but Seth had more than enough methods to dispose of him. He first needed to rid himself of his bindings, but he wasn't sure how robust the metal was and if he had any material strong enough to break it.

The Evodent bounced back and forth on the table and pivoted towards Seth.

"Do you know why you're here, boy?"

Seth, looking at his hands, sighed in resignation and looked at the officer on the table as he answered.

"No, but I am getting used to it."

The Evodent exhaled sharply.

"Well let me shed some light on the situation for you. Apparently someone down in Dewall was cut in half, at the same time as a human fitting your description was present. Now you are here, and we are hearing reports of Evodent property being vandalised in the same manner."

"Vandalism? I didn't do that either!" said Seth. He dropped his eyes back to the metal knotted around his wrists.

"How does this metal work? I've not seen anything like this before."

The Evodent had turned away slightly and gave Seth a sidelong glance as he spoke.

"You want to know the secrets of the incarceration staff? Think you can escape, huh? Well without years of training — and the other end of that staff — you will have a bit of trouble. I have never seen a human strong enough to break free from the pulse knot."

"What does the other end of the staff do?" Seth asked.

"Listen here boy! You left a trail of destruction from Dewall, through Jesterton, Thalls and False Hills, we know it was you! You did the same thing in Dewall! Only this time you restrained yourself from murdering and just ruined people's property. The chief in Dewall told us all about you, but it seems you aren't so powerful with your hands bound together. I could release you simply by pressing this button," — the Evodent indicated a button on the black part of a baton he was holding — "but Gary told me you would make fire come out of your hands? Is this right? Are you some sort of barrier-builder?"

Seth was not listening as he had already begun to project a small blue strand of stone towards the button on the Evodent's baton. The stone string tapped the button and the metal around his wrist uncoiled so fast it slapped his wrist, leaving a red line on his arm.

"Huh?" said the Evodent, looking puzzled at the blue stone fibre pushing against his staff, and following it with his eyes to Seth's finger. Now freed, Seth stood up, towering above the nervous being.

"Listen, I don't know exactly what is going on but I am not to blame. I am honestly trying to help. What is it you mean by a 'trail of destruction'?" Seth asked the trembling Evodent.

The small creature made a slight movement. Seth assumed he was about to perform some acrobatics like Gary had and instinctively raised his hand ready to defend himself. The Evodent decided not to attack and relaxed his stance when he saw Seth's raised hand.

"By 'a trail of destruction' I mean you sliced the place up, like you did poor Chris from Dewall. You sliced houses and fences in half and you destroyed a school — a straight line from one end to the other! Luckily no one was in your path this time."

The route through Jesterton, Thalls and False Hills sounded familiar to Seth. According to his map, he had actually flown over those precise villages on his floating concrete segment. And the other crime in Dewall happened after he had flown above the village too... he was starting to wonder if he actually *was* responsible. Every part of the villages he had been above had similar tales of destruction. As Seth was thinking the surrounding doors burst open revealing several more Evodents ready to advance upon him. Seth waved a hand and all the doors slammed back shut, mud rose from the ground in front of each entrance preventing the Evodents from entering the room. He could hear the small creatures thumping on the doors as he was thinking. Maybe the tornado he was using had some kind of side effect, but he hadn't noticed anything until now because he hadn't flown above anything that would be affected?

When Seth was on his segment he could see nothing of his personal tornado touching the ground, but it was possible that it was still there, so thin it was invisible to the naked eye. So thin, in fact, it could have caused the very damage of which he was being accused.

Uh oh, Seth thought. He had enough disturbing images haunting him since his confrontation in Chos Garren and *now* he was going to have to deal with the fact that he had killed an innocent farmer. He needed to be much more careful with his matter manipulation. Seth thought about the philosophy of the shadow arc's resistance, and decided honesty was the best policy right now, if only to alleviate his guilty conscience.

"Uuuhhh, there might be a problem here. I want to be honest; those houses, and Chris the farmer, were an accident." Seth said it so succinctly and without hesitation he surprised himself. The hand of the chief swung up to point at Seth.

"Aha!"

Seth scratched his head.

"But I want to make it good again. As much as I may deserve it, I don't think you will be able to enforce any punishment on me, but there must be some way I can help you. I mean, I can do a lot more than just cut things in half," he said to the Evodent pointing accusingly at Seth.

Eventually the Evodent standing on the table calmed down a little, his name turned out to be Ferrie, and at Ferrie's request he broke all the mud blockades holding the doors shut. Ferrie had to yell frantically to his men as they ran into the room to stand down. He ordered most of them to leave and then discussed what should be done with Seth, while a few angry Evodents stood alert around the room. Seth demonstrated several of his powers for Ferrie: the water propeller, waterscope, a spark jet, and an azurite seat, which Seth then sat down in, finding it better than the spot on the floor against the wall. The chief was unimpressed, but Ferrie came up with a somewhat elegant solution. The normal punishment for murder was a lifetime in the incarceration centre, but Ferrie thought Seth could at least spend some time getting to know the city and the Evodent civilization. At least he would be dedicating some time to repairing his misdeeds, and he would most likely find a better way to help the Evodents than just making sparks fly from his hand. So Seth decided he would spend some time here to discover what solutions his powers could provide to the Evodents. He also needed to investigate the melding phenomenon he had seen; he had had no idea the Evodents would be capable of matter manipulation too.

Seth began his education by asking different Evodents for advice, but no one wanted to talk to him. Ferrie had alerted the townspeople of Seth's intentions but apparently they couldn't get past the fact that he was a murderer and were mostly too scared to talk with him for longer than a few sentences. He couldn't blame them really; he hadn't killed anyone intentionally but he *had* still killed someone. Frustrated, Seth decided to take a break in the park he had seen earlier. He walked to the centre and saw that the melding was still in progress. The hostess was making strange gestures with her staff in front of the multicoloured tent. Seth sat down and found he was getting used to sitting on the ground.

The hostess spoke dramatically:

"And now that the trance has left Jessica and Kyle, they are free to start living their lives as bipeds! Everyone hold up your cards."

Hearing names other than Linda and Shaun, Seth realised this was a different melding; the park must be a common place to hold a melding. All of the Evodents sitting in rows raised up their cards, some with their actual hands while other used the hands on the end of their staffs.

Seth could not see what was on the cards but he heard the hostess react:

"Aww, what sweet messages. Now, the Domestic has already left to perform another melding but Jessica and Kyle are still a bit sensitive so they can't use their bipedal abilities fully quite yet. But they are melded, and won't be able to hear you, so hold your cards up high and the happily melded couple can see you will still be able to tell them how much they mean to you all!" The hostess opened the flap to the tent behind her. Two Evodents joined at the ear walked slowly out of the coloured tent. They stopped and smiled as they looked around at their fellow Evodents. Seth wasn't really sure what else he should have expected, already being privy to one melding process. He decided his attention would best be directed elsewhere, like where the Domestic had gone with his small sun-in-a-box.

Eventually Seth recognised two familiar, melded Evodents walking slowly; it was Linda and Shaun. Linda was crying, and Shaun didn't look happy at all — apparently their melding might have been a mistake. They looked at him with a glimmer of recognition in their eyes. Being handcuffed and taken away by ten police officers must have left quite an impression — and being the only human in Stique at the moment helped too. Seth opened his mouth but he remembered that this was pointless for melded Evodents. Seth paused for a second and the sad couple turned to walk away, but Seth held his hand up for them to stop. Shaun and Linda stopped and became distracted by what Seth had started doing with his hands. Seth's imagination was not so controlled that he could just project bits of stone into the shape of the words he needed, but it seemed to work well enough when he traced the letters with his index finger. In the air floated some blue letters saying "Why are you two so sad?". The blue letters fell softly into the dirt. From what Seth had witnessed, the act of melding was supposed to be something to celebrate.
The Evodent on the right closed his eyes, and the one on the left began speaking with a high-pitched voice.

"Sorry Shaun, but I never knew that Derek felt that way! I never pursued it because I...." Linda's words were cut off as her sobbing took over. Shaun opened his eyes again and looked at Seth. Tears were slowly trickling from both his eyes, but still he said nothing. Seth started writing in the air again: "Can't you unmeld?" The letters clunked off each other as they fell into the dirt. Linda began speaking so loud he was sure it was thundering in Shaun's head.

"No! Melding is forever! I can never be....with Derek — not like this. I'm sorry Shaun."

Seth frowned as he realised just how bad it must be for both of them: Linda could not show Derek that she loved him without causing Shaun pain. She could never have a relationship with poor Derek — and Derek probably couldn't stand the sight of Shaun either. And Shaun had no way of getting over Linda. She would be attached to his head, her voice the only audible thing in the world for the rest of their lives. Seth was curious as to what happened to them when one of them died of old age. Seth began writing in the air again with his finger but stopped himself. Time for a more pertinent question. With blue stone, Seth wrote in the air: "If I helped you would you be able to tell me about the barrier-builders and The Wandering Cross?" He actually had to start walking sideways to finish the question; he had not accounted for the physical length of the sentence. This time Shaun responded.

"I thought *you* were a barrier-builder. Only they could make something like those blue letters the way you do."

"Yes! Yes! I would help!" Linda said over him, jumping a little and causing Shaun to wince in pain as the still sensitive skin joining the two stretched a little.

Seth wrote the words "Where can we talk?" in the air and let them float for a few seconds before the letters all fell to the ground.

The trio had to find a place outside for their conversation. The Evodents had tried taking him to their home, but Seth couldn't crawl into the house without breaking something. It was nice to see the couple weren't crying anymore; Shaun seemed to be sulking a bit, but Linda was completely distracted by the possibility of being able to be with Derek, so his mood was understandable. The letters Seth was summoning had become neater, thinner and more stable, making their communication more efficient. His questioning had revealed that the Domestic knew just as much about matter manipulation as Shaun and Linda did, which was very little. The sun-in-a-box, known to the Evodents as a 'Melder', was actually an artefact left behind by the barrier-builders. It seemed a strange thing to Seth to leave such a specific artefact behind. But perhaps the barrier-builders were more focused on love than Seth initially thought; it began to seem a little less odd.

The barrier-builders were a man and a woman; their names were Faust and Trikala. There were many legends that circulated among the population of the Evodents; in all of them the two barrier-builders were shown to be compassionate, with a love between them that was so strong it would never be broken. Some Evodents said the barrier stayed up only because of Faust and Trikala's love. One of the things Red had told Seth was that anything that had survived the shockwave was most likely a creation of Jacobus and Iselle, the two element binders that had created Red.

Seth suspected that Jacobus and Iselle were also Faust and Trikala, although in Red's stories they were not so friendly with each other. But if that was the case, then he could definitely find something valuable in the knowledge they had left behind. It also explained how an Evodent was able to perform such intricate and controlled matter manipulation. Seth had gained respect for the Evodents, but he still found it hard to believe such strange, crutch-dependant creatures could manipulate matter on a higher level than him. He started to form his own plan to help the unhappily melded couple as they revealed more and more knowledge to him.

The barrier-builders had their own humongous temple known as The Wandering Cross, which very few Evodents had visited. The only way to reach The Wandering Cross was via pilgrimage. It was once a rite of passage for becoming a Domestic, but too many Evodents never returned, so the trial for becoming a Domestic was made a little more lenient. The journey from here to The Wandering Cross used to be perilous and long, but since the shockwave it had become perilous *because* it was long; when there was still vegetation, the Evodents were able to hunt and forage for food during their pilgrimage, but now there was nothing but barren waste between here and The Wandering Cross.

The Evodents travelled to the temple to learn skills from the barrier-builders, but that knowledge had been lost and the temple was now believed to be deserted. This "Wandering Cross" was definitely something Seth needed to investigate; Faust and Trikala had lived there in the early days of the Evodents. The two-barrier builders were even said to have created the Evodents in their efforts to express their endless compassion. But they were constant travellers. Many of the stories held references to Faust and Trikala travelling through places that could not be reached by traditional means. The Wandering Cross housed the actual manuscript where the complete story was written. Everything that was known in the villages of the Evodents was from the few pilgrims that had returned from The Wandering Cross.

Seth needed to know how to get to this temple. Now that he knew where the knowledge of this village originated, he had a direction to go. Already Seth's mind was starting to come up with plans on how to find it. The stories didn't paint it as a small structure, and if it was reachable by Evodents it couldn't be too far, considering their average stride length. The temple was sure to hold plenty of useful knowledge to assist Seth in becoming a better matter manipulator. His plan was fairly simple; he was going to ask Shaun and Linda in which general direction The Wandering Cross lay, then fly as high as he could on his concrete vessel while watching the ground for any cross shapes — or anything, really.

Linda was waiting patiently while Seth stared up at the sky, thinking about his plan to soon be soaring through the air. She cleared her throat somewhat exaggeratedly to get Seth's attention. He hadn't spoken for the last ten seconds and it was starting to become awkward. He shook his head as Linda's throat clearing brought him back to ground level. He looked down at the sad couple and remembered he had also agreed to help these two somehow. Since seeing the strange mini sun-in-a-box, Seth had been thinking of how he could make something similar, but creating a star was most likely not something he could achieve yet. And what exactly would he *do* with the star? How was it responsible for the melding process?

Linda finally spoke.

"You know we were warned not to associate with you. They said you are, umm, cutting people in half."

Shaun looked up slightly at hearing this. His complexion paled slightly as he thought about the poor Evodent's life he had taken. He started instinctively to apologise, but realised he needed to continue writing sentences in the air: "Sorry, it was an accident, I honestly had no idea I was doing it," wrote Seth. Shaun looked concerned now.

"Umm, honey, I don't think we should be –"

"Don't call me honey Shaun, this man is going to help both of us and we won't have to pretend to like each other anymore — sorry again, but Derek's confession really changed everything," Linda snapped brashly, causing Shaun to wince a little. Seth was curious as to what the small homunculus was referring; surely she didn't think he was going to cut them apart.

"You're going to cut us apart!" proclaimed Linda loudly, proud of herself for coming up with such an ingenious solution.

Seth almost laughed out loud before he began writing his response in the air: "Are you kidding? Surely that has been tried before? You might die," he wrote, with a much more serious expression on his face.

"I think it will be different. You are a barrier-builder too. I just know if you did it, it will be alright." The small female Evodent was practically pleading with him. Seth believed her idea was based on a mistaken belief. "I am not a barrier-builder" he traced out in blue stone. "You might die! I don't want to kill anyone". Linda dropped to her knee, pulling Shaun down with her and she held her hand out, palm upwards. Tears were starting to well up in her eyes again.

"Please! If you cannot separate us I don't want to live anyway! I cannot go through life this way. Why would you be so cruel?"

"I am not cruel; you are being cruel to Shaun. He melded with you!" blue stone materialised along the path Seth's finger traced. Linda began speaking again before he had finished writing.

"Please Seth! You have to do this. It is the only way for any of us to be happy again!"

Every comment Linda made like this caused Shaun to wince slightly. Seth became angry about how tactless she was being to the Evodent that had willingly given up his freedom for his love for her. "Shut up Linda", wrote Seth, causing Linda to gasp but she held her tongue and Seth thought quickly about what he would write. "Everything you are doing and saying now hurts Shaun. At this point it would help him more than you."

Now Linda was looking just as depressed as Shaun. Both of them were still on their knees.

"I don't want to live either way. Linda, you were my whole life! Without you I don't know what I'm going to do," said Shaun, without looking up. Linda started crying too, Seth really wanted to help them. He desperately tried to think of a solution.

"Stop!" he suddenly shouted, then reverted back to his increasingly neat blue stone handwriting: "Stop, I will try." Linda stopped crying and looked up at Seth.

"R-really? You'll do it? I just know it will work!"

Seth very much had his doubts, but if he was successful this may be the solution that redeemed him for Chris' death — either that, or there would be two more dead… Shaun still looked skeptical.

"Uhhh, I don't think this is the best idea. Maybe we should do this with a Domestic present."

Despite Shaun saying how little he cared to live, he had made a very valid, possibly life-saving point. So the three of them decided to give it a proper try. If Linda's plan didn't work at least they would have someone with medical knowledge nearby to prevent too much damage. Shaun and Linda knew how to contact a Domestic easily. It took about five minutes for them to reach him: the Domestic was at home inside his dry mud hut when they found him. Apparently he had no more meldings to perform today and was free to help with this "demelding". The Domestic had his doubts about it, which he repeatedly mentioned, but Linda's conviction and persistence made him acquiesce. The Domestic also agreed that if this was going to happen either way, it would be better if he were present.

They assembled just outside his home, and Seth tried creating a small tornado. He hoped he wouldn't need to create one as high as the tornado that had been slicing up the Evodent's houses and carrying him across the barren landscape of the world. A tiny grey cone appeared about two metres above the ground in front of Seth, its surface rippling as the wind in the miniature tornado spun rapidly. A small grey line extended down towards the ground — and then the tornado disappeared.

Seth looked a little disappointed and tried again. He created five more tornados until finally he was able to maintain a stable one. Just like the wind that supported his home high above the

planet's surface, the lowest part of the tornado was invisible to the naked eye. Hopefully it was stable enough to stay spinning while Linda and Shaun passed under it. There was a lot of dust flying in the air and Seth could hear it crunching in his mouth as he brought his teeth together. Linda and Shaun were staring towards their impending separation, either from each other or from the living world. The Domestic was sweating, unnerved by the idea of the serious injuries he assumed he would soon have to attempt to repair.
Seth looked at Linda and Shaun. No one had really spoken for a while, all of them lost in their thoughts: Linda thought of her incipient freedom from Shaun, Shaun thought about his impending release from sorrow, and Seth was thinking about how much death he had seen since he started his journey.

Seth materialised a horizontal rod of dried mud about fifty centimetres long and caught it with one had. He then threw the dried mud towards the mini whirlwind; the rod was cut with a perfectly straight incision by an unseen force. Everyone gasped as they saw how easily the mud had been sliced. Shaun and Linda's skin was quite pale to begin with, but they seemed to lose what little colour they had when they saw this and the reality of what they were about to do. However scared the freshly melded pair looked they still had the bravery to start walking forwards. Even though the tornado was tiny it was still stirring up enough wind to make it difficult for Shaun and Linda to progress. Linda held up her hand trying to shield her eyes from the dust flying through the air, the two were visibly leaning forward now. Shaun had lifted his hand up to stop the dust ruining his vision too. Seth easily maintained the small tornado — he been manipulating one at least fifty times this size the past month — but he was holding his breath wondering what would happen. The bottom half of the column of wind was invisible, but the Evodents could see where it was: a subtle dot of coning

FALLEN WORLD

dirt appeared in the ground where the tornado bore into the ground. Everyone was now holding their breath as Linda and Shaun approached the whirlwind.

The cut was so small no one had noticed it happening, but suddenly Shaun and Linda were moving further and further apart; it looked like it had actually worked. Blood spilled out from Linda's fresh wound, but Shaun had very little blood to show for the mini operation that had just been performed. The Domestic quickly hopped over to Linda and began applying a dressing to her wound. Shaun attempted to help; the string of wind must have cut more into Linda's tiny body than Shaun's.

The Domestic stood up and looked at Seth after he had stopped Linda's bleeding.

"I cannot believe that actually worked. You really are a barrier-builder. This has never been done before!"

Seth was completely speechless. There was no way that should have worked — if it was that easy surely the Evodents would have done this already.

"The incision was so clean it barely ruptured any veins or arteries, and maybe since their melding was so fresh they hadn't really created any vital pathways yet. This is a huge step in Evodent technology," said the Domestic to Seth excitedly.

Linda was now unconscious. Shaun was looking at her with concern on his face, something Seth personally could not understand, considering what Linda had been saying and doing in the past hours. The Domestic reassured Seth that she would be ok; her blood loss was minimal, and Evodent red blood cell production was very efficient. Soon she would be back to her pale green colour once more. Shaun looked relieved that she was going to be ok. Seth thought that if he was Shaun, he would be happy to see her gone — but then, he had never loved anyone so much that he wanted to be physically attached to them for the rest of his life. Shaun was going to have some trouble adjusting, Seth was sure, but it would certainly be much easier to move on without Linda attached to him.

FALLEN WORLD

Chapter 12

Seth was back in the air, cruising above the empty dirt landscape that was now his home. He had traced a very specific course as he had left the network of villages where the Evodents resided. Despite the tragic instances that occurred while he was there (and his multiple run-ins with the authorities) he was a little sorry to go. The people of Stique had mixed feelings about Seth now too. He had killed someone — which was made public — and had refused to accept the normal punishment — which was also made public. But he had ended up greatly helping Evodent society; introducing demelding meant great changes for the Evodents. Some people did not even want to make eye contact with a murderer, while other Stique citizens wanted to shake his hand for allowing them to finally separate from their irritating significant others.

It felt like a hollow victory; despite Seth's inexperience with the phenomenon of love, he understood that someone could make a mistake with his discovery, but it seemed like even the *possibility* of demelding had gotten a lot of Evodents excited. Now there would be less love within the Evodent society. Seth was happy to provide them with the choice, however. Melding was already quite a drastic move, even without being permanent; he completely understood any Evodents that would want to return to unipedal locomotion.

Linda had completely lost her hearing during the demelding, while Shaun's was greatly reduced, but he was still able to communicate the old-fashioned way. Shaun told Seth the correct heading to find The Wandering Cross and Seth returned to his segment to begin his flight.

The small tornado he had summoned (nicknamed 'The Demelder') maintained itself easily without Seth: the atoms he had agitated to spin the tiny tornado stayed that way, even when he wasn't actively using his matter manipulation. After seeing the small star the Domestic was using, Seth was sure he could find a way to make his miniature whirlwind permanent. The answer was surprisingly simple: just leave it alone. Whenever Seth had docked his concrete ship he had always consciously willed the whirlwind to be still. He was always afraid that if he did let the tornado continue without his supervision, his segment would be smashed into the ground.

Seth flew along at a brisk pace, making sure that there was nothing below him that could be accidentally cut in half. While travelling, he tried to think of a new method of flying that stopped him from having to worry about such problems. He travelled east; according to Shaun he would find the Temple in this direction, if it wasn't destroyed by the shockwave. Seth assumed he would at the very least find some remains, since it was supposed to be a creation from Jacobus and Iselle —- or Faust and Trikala. Either way, it was definitely made by someone with extremely impressive matter manipulation skills.

The sky was clear and blue; just a few wisps of condensed water could be seen far off in the distance. The light brown dirt beneath Seth's segment stretched out beyond the horizon, occasionally broken up with the grey colour of stone. There seemed to be tiny dots of green scattered across the ground nowadays. The world was recovering from the great shockwave that had decimated its surface. Seth thought about how resilient a planet must be. Just one month ago there was no trace of life anywhere apart from the Evodents, yet small signs of life poked through the dusty brown soil everywhere. Right now the regolith was mainly inert soil, but where there was the even slightest bit of nutrition to be found, life grabbed hold and exploited it to its full advantage.

Red had told Seth that a planet should be treated as a living thing. Like everything, it was also made up of smaller parts, and a planet being so monumental in size made the smaller parts that contrived the gigantic ball of life much more apparent. Even Seth played a role in the make-up of the planet he was now floating above. If only *his* role were removed, it would not be so detrimental; like on the planets making up the elementals, one person less would not affect the ultimate outcome. His mind drifted back to the cyclical logic he had ascertained about the universe while existing at sub-atomic size. The particles making up the world of Estever, the sub-atoms, seemed to have a different mode of existence, more like the orbit of a system of planets.

When Seth was on Estever, he found the sub-atoms were not susceptible to any kind of matter manipulation. Evidently, something about the planet-beings, the elementals, was providing him with his power. He had also noticed the strange strands of lightning connecting the enormous atoms where the elementals lived; its shape reminded him of how certain columns of matter would manifest themselves. Maybe it was that lightning, bonding the atoms together, which was the main source of Seth's power... although it did not explain why the molten metal essence he had captured earlier in his adventure had influenced his physical size. Now, after seeing a tiny star kept in a small box by strange creatures, Seth realised there was a lot about matter manipulation he didn't understand. Red had said that Jacobus and Iselle had referred to their powers as element binding; maybe this was because of the role the elementals played in matter manipulation. Seth still insisted on calling it matter manipulation, although he was beginning to believe that element binding might actually be a more accurate term... *something* with 'elements' anyway. Maybe his discoveries at The Wandering Cross would reveal a decisive reason to call it 'element binding' — but Seth decided there were more important things to worry about.

The people now floating in Seth's old home city of Swevender were probably struggling by now. Everyone was able to fit on the central segment without too much trouble, but without their homes and gardens, they would have to hope that their surplus harvests would last long enough. They could even start growing new vegetables and fruit if they wanted, but the livestock had most likely floated down to the surface, trapped on their segments. They were probably starving, or lost in the endless dirt sea. Seth had heard stories of people going on adventures before, although they mostly were confined to a setting similar to Swevender. The people there had never seen any other way to exist, so their creativity was hindered somewhat. Seth knew now that they had all been greatly romanticised; his journey was filled with death and sadness. Some parts had been great, yes, but his travels had given him memories he would love to instantly forget. It was almost overwhelming how much bigger the world was than just Swevender, and discovering the good also meant discovering the bad.

Seth still liked to use the waterscope while standing at the bow of his floating concrete ship. As usual, it revealed a featureless dirt plain as far as he could see. Seth scanned carefully from left to right. Sometimes he would pull the water scope away from his eye to inspect the landscape for any anomalies that his tunnel vision might have missed. Seth was frequently disappointed.

He had expected the distance an Evodent could travel on foot wouldn't be any further than he could fly in a day, but the blue sky had started to darken and Seth was feeling tired. He felt that his tornado was descending slowly as he gradually lost the focus required to maintain his ship's normal altitude. Seth decided he should give the unipedal creatures a bit more credit and get some rest. He had not even been travelling a full day and he was already feeling tired — and this pilgrimage was referred to as long and perilous. Seth performed his usual evening rituals. He sat down just outside the small rainforest he still liked to maintain manually. His seat was manipulated from vines and was surprisingly soft. With a full belly, Seth's neck let his head fall limply forward... his body jerked suddenly as he woke from his half-second slumber. He stood up and made his way to bed, the ship docked on its usual column of dirt. His mind insisted on showing him the usual disturbing images that would keep him awake for the next hour while he lay in bed.

***

The next morning brought another sunny, cloudless day. Seth had a sudden epiphany as he got out of bed: he could try his water propeller to elevate his segment to Swevender's altitude. It was strange that he hadn't thought of it before, but Seth had been so wrapped up in his new abilities to control new kinds of matter he had forgotten the obvious solution. He quickly ate some sweet fruits for breakfast, then walked to the edge of his segment. He inspected the landscape further east through his water scope and saw a complete lack of anything significant. It was time to elevate his home higher than he ever had before. The solid column of dirt beneath his segment started to crumble as spinning blades of water manifested themselves inside of it and began spinning faster and faster. The blades had begun poking out of the cylinder of dirt but were already spinning so fast they were just a blur. Seth dramatically raised both his hands, palms up, as he willed his segment skywards. He wondered exactly why he needed to pose like that — there was no one around to watch him, and even without his dramatic posture what he was doing would have impressed onlookers anyway. Slowly, the small specks of green in the dirt below dwindled away and became part of the brown ground as the segment rose.

Seth started to feel cold. He wasn't quite sure at what altitude the clouds usually lay, but he believed he could now elevate himself there. Finally, his journey had brought him a step closer to Swevender — although now he had begun to think that if he were to make it back, he would prefer to journey the surface of the planet rather than live in the confines of the floating city again. In fact, Seth would probably reveal the truth about the world to everyone and encourage them all to do the same. Of course they would want to explore too; their only reason for staying in Swevender so long was blissful ignorance; nothing would stop them once they had the right knowledge. It got extremely cold as Seth went higher and he was having trouble breathing now. He decided this would best be tried when there were more clouds; he would know what altitude was appropriate — and maybe one of the clouds would be Swevender itself.

Feeling pleased, Seth slowly lowered his segment. The whirring of the huge propeller beneath him was the only thing he could hear. As he descended he noticed a small anomaly in the distance. At first he thought he was looking back at an Evodent village, but, noting the position of the sun he realised he was still facing east. Seth held up his hands and his waterscope appeared in them. He peered through it and sure enough, finally saw something in the distance apart from flat dirt or stone. He still couldn't quite make it out, but he was sure he had finally discovered The Wandering Cross.
Seth angled his propeller to drift towards the indistinguishable object. He heard loud crashing noises come from his house as everything fell out of cupboards and off shelves to rest against a wall that had suddenly become a little horizontal. Seth straightened the propeller out and descended slowly. When he could see he was level with the top of the dirt column that had supported his home overnight, he manifested his faithful old

tornado and started flying towards what he hoped was The Wandering Cross. Seth could no longer see the temple from his current height, even with the water scope, but he knew in exactly which direction to fly. The mess waiting for him inside the house could wait; he needed to find what secrets the distant temple held.

A small imperfection appeared in the horizon as The Wandering Cross was revealed again. Seth peeked through his waterscope. The temple had a lot more plants growing around it than the rest of the landscape. It certainly wasn't green, but the plants that had managed to grow were significantly bigger than in the surrounding landscape. He saw three arch-shaped tunnels made of big mud bricks. Two of the tunnels ran along the ground perpendicular to one another, forming a cross, while the third corridor pointed straight up from the intersection of the two crossed tunnels — basically an upright cylinder made of bricks. Only one of the openings facing Seth was visible, and Seth could see that there were hundreds of tiny rectangular objects inside the small tunnel. There also seemed to be some movement just outside the entrance to the corridor. Whatever was causing it was too small to see, but Seth would know soon enough. He let his waterscope dissipate into mist and continued his approach.

Slowly, Seth's concrete vessel approached the cross-shaped temple. The closer Seth came to the brick structure, the more intricate the details he was able to discern. The first thing he noticed was that the movement he had seen was actually a person, and if he was right it was a woman, or a man wearing extremely ornate clothing. Judging by the height of the woman, the corridor was about four to five metres tall, and the rectangular objects Seth had seen were doors, although not all were rectangles. None of them were attached to anything — in fact, they all seemed to be floating a few centimetres from the ground without any obvious purpose. Some of the doors had extremely elaborate frames; some, ornate door knockers. Other doors were made of perfectly flat steel, some looked old and used with rust creeping across its surface. Some of the wooden doors were infested with mould and rot. The doors were mostly in rows four across. Depending on the average size of the apertures, the amount of rows was impossible to judge, extending so far that they became indistinguishable.

Some of the tunnels containing the doors had suffered dilapidation, maybe from the shockwave or maybe just over time, but several bricks were cracked or had fallen, making a small opening that opened onto the interior of the tunnels. Outside the structure between the passageways were a lot more rocks and plants than on the rest of the barren surface Seth had been exploring. There were still relatively few plants but these ones must have had their rate of growth increased somehow and had grown to a formidable size; no trees, only extremely healthy bushes, currently adding a little colour to the landscape. Most were a dark green and any flowers that had managed to bloom were black. The bricks making up the structure were huge and thick. It would have taken a lot of manpower (or matter manipulation) to build the temple.

Seth parked his concrete ship on a column of dirt about two hundred metres from the entrance to the closest corridor, the same one he had seen the woman hanging about near. She was still outside, kneeling on the ground, tending to the plants. She spotted Seth approaching and stood up. She was wearing a rather puffy outfit with complex decorations. The dress was a pale pink colour and looked like it had at one point been a much more saturated shade. The dress was made of three layers, each one shorter than the last, with intricate white lace hanging from the bottom of each layer, the lowest of which was almost dragging on the ground. The woman's torso was clothed in the same motif of pale pink with white frills. The dress puffed out around her shoulders and elbows and she had a high collar surrounding the back of her long, slender neck. She had dark shiny hair tied back extremely tightly into a long braid half the length of her body. She looked like she was in her early thirties or late twenties, with a round face, a small round nose, and large eyes with extremely long lashes. She had two full lips and a somewhat large forehead.

Seth was only twenty metres from the woman when he yelled out to her.

"Hello!"

The woman yelled a greeting back to Seth and walked towards him.

"Hi, you must be Trikala, I heard about you from the Evodents" Seth said to her. She smiled and shook her head.

"Wow, I haven't heard that name for a long time. I thought the Evodents were gone; we haven't seen them for many years now. But no, I am not Trikala. My name is Jacquelyn, and who might you be?" she asked as he took in the worn, elaborate dress. Seth smiled, happy with such an amicable response.

"I am Seth. So... Trikala is somewhere in the temple then?"

Jacquelyn laughed before she answered.

"Sort of. Well, not really... first of all, it's not a temple, but the last time I saw her she was heading inside."

Seth was confused and the look on his face revealed it."

"Wait, is this The Wandering Cross? The Evodents told me Trikala was inside the temple called The Wandering Cross."

"That is what the Evodents called it, but it's not a temple. To them it was something similar, but none of them have ever actually been inside to pray or whatever it is they wanted to do, so how would they know anyway?" replied Jacquelyn, somewhat dismissively.

Still uncertain, Seth decided to keep inquiring.

"You said 'we'. Who else is here, Faust?"

FALLEN WORLD

Jacquelyn looked behind her at the rows and rows of doors then back at Seth and she opened her mouth to answer.

"Heidi, my sister. You might meet her, although I haven't seen her for years. Faust, I haven't seen for even longer. What are you doing here Seth? Don't tell me you are going on the Evodent pilgrimage to become a Domestic. I thought the Evodents didn't even like humans."

Seth raised his hands in a halting gesture so he could explain his purpose.

"It's a longer story really, but basically my home fell because of the great shockwave and now I am trying to get back there. I recently learnt a lot more matter manipulation but not enough to get home. I figured that if Trikala or Faust were here they could help me somehow."

This time Jacquelyn laughed very hard, preventing her from answering until she had finished chuckling.

"They would not help you. They do not care about anyone anymore. The idea they would teach you is laughable, and not only that, but you want to learn to become more powerful, something that would threaten their position in this universe. I think you definitely have things to learn though. First of all, it's called element binding, and judging by the primitive method you were using to fly here, you haven't grasped even a fraction of it. Who taught you that, by the way?"

Now Seth was getting somewhere. He may not have found Faust or Trikala but he had found someone who knew something about matter manipulation, so he answered honestly hoping to learn something from this irritating woman.

"I learned it from a creature called Red. He lives in the Restyard. Now, what do you know about element binding?" Seth asked, hoping he was still sounding friendly. Jacquelyn looked surprised.

"You were in the Restyard? Wow, maybe you do know more than a fraction. What I know about element binding is extensive but I'm not here to teach you about that; I'm here to show you the way."

Once again Seth's face expressed confusion.

"What way?"

"The way to the bridge of the ship, Seth. Trust me, you won't make it without my help." Jacquelyn gestured towards the corridor filled with mysterious doors. Seth looked towards the strange hallway of doors. One of them was broken and a strange green light crept through the small cracks in the door. The corridor seemed to go on forever. Behind all of the doors, an ambient light cast eerie shadows on the ground and walls of the corridor.

Originally, Seth thought he would find two welcoming element binders, judging by the stories the Evodents had presented Seth with, but this was something completely unexpected. Jacquelyn was extremely sure of herself, to the point of being annoying, but she clearly knew things Seth did not. Her reaction to the Restyard showed she was familiar with Jacobus, Iselle and element binding, but she only wanted to show Seth to the centre of the building — which was apparently a ship. *If it's a ship*, Seth thought, *it might help me reach Swevender*. Although he couldn't imagine such a huge structure flying, but again Jacquelyn showed that she was in possession of unique knowledge and could most likely help him.

Jacquelyn smiled at the confusion on Seth's face. He couldn't understand exactly why this woman would help him, especially just for one very specific purpose. Until just now, Seth did not even know that The Wandering Cross was a ship, and now this woman wanted to show Seth to the centre of it — something he was quite sure he could do just by flying, but he was curious as to the purpose of all the doors.

"Why wouldn't I make it without your help? And what's at the bridge of the ship?" Seth asked the obvious question that Jacquelyn was clearly waiting for. Her smile grew even wider.

On someone else, Seth would have found it pleasant, but on Jacquelyn it just made him dislike her even more.

"Aha!" Jacquelyn raised her finger, getting ready for an obviously rehearsed rhetoric;
"In the centre of the bridge lies more knowledge than you could imagine, young Seth. Trikala and Faust may not be here anymore, but what they left behind is something you could not even begin to comprehend. This ship does not travel like other ships; it moves through *universes*. No matter how much you have seen of this world, it is only fraction of what is yet to be discovered. If I lead you through the specific pattern of doors you will arrive at the bridge, the control centre of... 'The Wandering Cross' as you and the Evodents call it."
Seth's eyes grew larger and larger during Jacquelyn's little sales pitch. Whatever this ship was, it was more than he had expected. He thought he might find a ruined temple with tiny remnants of stories or references to element binding. At the most he expected one of the element binders to be there. But this long corridor filled with strange doors, guarded by an irritating lady wearing fancy old clothes? This was not what he had expected.
Seth thought a little bit.

"Could I not just walk in between the doors?"
Jacquelyn still had a smirk on her face when she answered.

"Anyone can walk between the doors. Anyone can walk into that door —," Jacquelyn pointed to an ornate door with a brass frame of intricate floral designs, slightly oxidised, "— but it will produce no results. Reaching the bridge is no simple matter, and I am here to help you, Seth."
The ornate door was only a few metres away and looked like the most welcoming ingress from the first row of doors. Seth decided he would open it as Jacquelyn had suggested, curious what results he might produce. Seth walked casually to the door and grabbed the handle which was cold and made from brass. He turned it, and the door flew open with incredible force, knocking

Seth aside. From the open door burst a torrent of water. Luckily, the door had pushed Seth out of the path of the powerful deluge. He stood up and stared at the incredible quantity of water now spilling over the parched landscape. There were some coloured objects visible in the water — strange creatures Seth had never seen before. Small orange, diamond-shaped animals bounced around in the still water. Some of them had black and white stripes breaking the pure orange colour and their skin was slightly reflective. The landscape in front of the door was becoming a huge pool of mud as the water flowed endlessly forth. It would soon be a lake if it continued much longer.

Seth fired a powerful gust of wind to try forcing the door shut, but the strength of the flowing water was too much for him. He began shouting as he increased the air flow and the door slowly closed. Just as the door shut the last stem of water had been directed straight towards Jacquelyn, blocking her from view with an explosion of water. Seth expected to see an irritated, angry, soaking woman once the water had washed away but she was standing in a small circle completely devoid of any sign of dampness, still with the familiar arrogant smirk on her face.

"So. I am still offering to help you. Getting to the centre is not a simple matter," Jacquelyn said calmly to Seth, looking towards the oasis of mud that Seth had just created.

Seth walked towards another door. This one was much simpler: a plain rectangle shape with a dark green painted wooden frame. The door was made of vertical planks about ten centimetres wide. The metal handle was the fanciest part of the door, with a small curve that ended in a delicate spiral. Seth cautiously opened it. Light poured from the crack as the door stood slightly ajar. Feeling no pressure against the wooden door, Seth opened it a little further. He looked into the aperture. The door led to a very different landscape: the light had a much more yellow tint, and there were patches of grass dotting the ground. Trees with an extremely bright red bark extended into the sky, with very few leaves to block the yellow sunlight. The landscape was quite flat and there seemed to be a field of doors with the same inconsistent design as The Wandering Cross.

Seth peered through the open door and looked back to Jacquelyn.

"So these doors lead back here?"

A small chuckle emerged from Jacquelyn's lips.

"No."

A short silence followed. Seth expected her to elaborate but clearly Jacquelyn was happy to leave it at a monosyllable. Seth's hand was still on the handle of the open door when the landscape inside the door showed a sign of movement. Seth stared. The movement was something off in the distance, growing larger as it came closer. It was a four-legged beast that had nothing friendly to its appearance. Its four legs rippled with muscles as it ran towards Seth, its skin a dark blue and its paws tipped with razor-sharp black claws that gleamed as it raised its legs to take an enormous stride. The head of the thing was a huge lump in the front of its horizontal torso, with angry, pitch-black eyes. Its mouth seemed to be permanently open; a ring of jagged teeth pointed downwards and an incredible amount of drool was spilling from the orifice as the creature thundered forwards. It had almost reached Seth and he moved to close the door, but he noticed that all the other doors in the distance were actually still in *front* of the behemoth, meaning the beast still had a lot of distance to cover before it reached him. It must have been comparable in size to a small mountain! One of the red trees broke in half as the creature smashed through it, not even slowing down. Seth closed the door hastily.

He decided he would try one more door before giving in. This third door had a featureless metal surface and was so shiny it was almost a mirror. It was made of three square panels, each one with small metal knobs dotting their circumferences. There was no door handle this time, so Seth pushed on the flat surface.

Nothing happened. He stepped back and noticed the frame of the door had a small silver button — it was possible this door led somewhere with technology similar to what the Inquirers possessed. The idea the Inquirers might be behind the door made Seth hesitate. Images of a dimly lit room filled with dead bodies briefly invaded his imagination. He took a deep breath and pressed the button. The door slid open and revealed a well-lit room.

Nothing was inside the small white room but one man in a chair facing Seth. He was wearing simple grey clothes. His hands were behind him, and he was slumped in the chair with his head hanging loosely. He tilted his head upwards slowly and eventually made eye contact with Seth. It took a few seconds for the long-haired man to react, but when he did, his eyes widened and he started screaming.

"NOOOO! You're not here!"

Seth wasn't sure how to react, he didn't quite understand the principle of the doors so it was possible that he was, in fact, not there.

"Ummm," Seth started to speak and the man began struggling in his chair. He kicked at the ground, knocking himself and the chair over onto the floor.

From a side of the room Seth couldn't see came three larger men in dark blue clothing. One of them grabbed the man and sat him straight up again. The man struggled, screaming "nooo!" the whole time. A voice from an unknown source could be heard:

"He's having another episode, sedate him."

One of the men in the blue uniforms glanced towards Seth. He looked just as surprised as the screaming man in the chair.

"Huh?" Said the larger man as he noticed Seth standing there staring at him. Seth quickly hit the door's button and it flew shut. Seth wasn't sure why he did that; there didn't seem to be any real danger, but he just had the idea that he was not supposed to be there. None of the doors had yielded any rewards.

Seth was ready to give up. He looked towards Jacquelyn who stood with arms akimbo and an arrogant smirk.

Chapter 13

The interior of The Wandering Cross was quite simple: a long, straight corridor with an arched roof led to the centre of the 'temple'. Seth had flown above all of the doors to the middle of the space and judged the length of the hallway to be about three hundred metres. The centre was a dome with five huge passageways running in perpendicular directions; one lead upwards and the sky could be seen at the end of the circular tunnel with hundreds of doors floating skywards in horizontal rows. The other four hallways were the same as the one that had brought Seth here, to where he thought the bridge should be. Seth flew through all four other corridors and found no notable differences. All of them had walls made of gigantic mud bricks, some of which had fallen away or crumbled, all of them filled with rows and rows of doors. All the doors apparently led somewhere dangerous, or just nonsensical; Seth had encountered universes so small only one finger could fit through its door. One door contained pure nothingness — when it opened the darkness inside seemed so powerful and deep that it sucked the light out of the surrounding air. Inside almost every single door, Seth found another field of eclectically decorated doors.

Once he was was satisfied that he had looked thoroughly through the five corridors (he didn't open *every* door of course, after some of them revealed worlds that Seth was sure would bring nothing but a quick and painful death), he returned to the entrance where Jacquelyn was waiting. She still had that annoying grin on her face, but Seth had to concede: he had explored enough of The Wandering Cross to see that there was no way of getting anywhere without the very real risk of being eternally lost in a maze of doors.

"So, have you found the bridge yet?" asked Jacquelyn.

Seth took a long pause after he floated to the ground near her. This woman was making it impossible to accept any help from her. Jacquelyn took Seth's silence as an admission of the negative and she spoke once again.

"Ok, so I am here to help you –"
Seth interrupted her.
"But why?"
She looked at Seth.

"How am I supposed to know? So, I know the route. It's not short, or safe, so I hope you have your... "matter manipulation" up to scratch, because I guarantee you will need it," and she started walking.

Seth followed her as she moved between the doors. She advanced three rows and stopped. Seth turned sideways to fit between two ornate doors in the third row and was now standing next to Jacquelyn.

She looked at Seth with the most serious expression than she had worn since she had met him.

"By the way, you can call me Jacqui if you prefer. Your journey starts here," Jacqui gestured towards a red wooden door behind Seth. Seth turned around, slowly grabbed the handle, looked at Jacqui and then back to the door. He was about to turn the handle but then a door to his left opened and Jacqui's head poked out. Confused, Seth turned back to the Jacqui that had just told him which door to open and she now had a very angry look on her face. The head poking out of the door must have been Heidi. It spoke first:

"Do not, open that! You will die, Heidi! Why do you want to destroy this place?"

And the first Jacqui started laughing maniacally. She raised her hand with a palm towards Seth and a small green glow appeared. Seth had no idea what was happening, but he sensed danger. He stood ready to fly out of harm's way if necessary. The second

Jacqui, head was still poking out of a simple black door, grabbed Seth and pulled him through the open frame.

Seth did not feel any transition as the world around him flickered from one to another. He landed on hard black ground, and saw the place he had just been standing on the other side of the open door was replaced by a huge green beam of light, the same colour as Seth just saw appearing in the first Jacqui's hand. Surrounding Seth was a strange black world. Trees with no leaves were scattered across the landscape, all coloured pure black. There seemed to be a strong sun in this world and the ground was hot to the touch. Seth lifted himself a few centimetres from the ground, already feeling its heat through his sandals. The landscape was full with hills and forests of black leafless trees and hundreds of doors. The sun was the only thing that wasn't black besides the doorway behind Seth, which still stood open.

While Seth was scanning the landscape around him he noticed Jacqui standing next to him looking slightly panicked.

"What just happened?" Seth asked Jacqui — or Heidi, he wasn't sure.

"My sister Heidi just tried to kill you, and I saved you. Believe me, opening that other door would have meant instant death," answered... Jacqui. Seth decided more questions were in order.

"Why would she kill me?"

The panicked look on Jacqui's face had not yet faded, and she responded hastily.

"Look, I can tell you soon, but we need to get you away from this door and towards that one," and she pointed towards a door in the distance. Seth wasn't entirely sure which since they were all the same black colour, but he knew which direction to go.

FALLEN WORLD

A great glowing green hand with foot long sharp claws shot through the open doorway and grabbed Jacqui.

"GO! I can't help you if she gets through!" she yelled at Seth. The green hand looked like it was squeezing something. Dark green smoke rose from the hand and emerald coloured fire could be seen flickering between huge the fingers. Jacqui was screaming, not in pain but more like a battle cry. A pink light appeared inside the hand, making it slightly translucent. The light grew stronger and stronger and darkened to a blood-red. Suddenly the build-up of energy caused the hand to fly open, and the ensuing force knocked Seth backwards for several metres.

"GO NOW!" screamed Jacqui as the green hand retracted back through the open door.

Seth felt sure that getting away from these two bewildering women was the right option and started flying towards the door Jacqui had indicated. Another glowing green hand shot past Seth towards the same door for which he was heading. Less than a second passed when a pure white blade of light appeared and sliced the hand loose at the wrist. The green hand was significantly smaller than the first Seth had seen, and it dissipated before it hit the ground. He continued to fly towards the black door, looking backwards occasionally in case more green hands came to pluck him from the air. It was now obvious which door Jacqui had meant: the other structures around it were actually tree stumps. From a distance, it was hard to determine in this strange, silhouetted landscape. When Seth landed he paused to turn around and observe the battle between these two sisters. One was glowing red all over and bolts of red lightning could be seen discharging from her glowing body. The other was waving her giant green plasma hand around. A second green hand extended from her other palm — towards Seth. He saw the hand grow in size as it approached him, and it was clear that whoever controlled these green hands wanted him dead.

The idea that the door he was about to enter may also contain instant death was in the back of Seth's mind; he couldn't help hesitating about whether or not to open it. *None* of the doors in this landscape looked like they contained anything good. Seth created a wall of magnesium that dug deep into the ground between him and the glowing green hand flying towards him. He then clicked his fingers and fired a cone of sparks towards his magnesium wall, using the ensuing fire to create a bright white blaze in his palm. The green hand elevated its trajectory so it could fly over the wall Seth had created. As it got nearer, it angled downwards, towards Seth. The flame in Seth's hand grew expansively and engulfed the green hand. Seth projected a huge arc of fire, widening to fifty metres at the far end. The glowing appendage slowed down as it struggled to maintain cohesion in the torrent of hot white fire. It broke apart and dispersed into hundreds of bits of green plasma before disappearing. Seth maintained his blazing torrent for several more seconds, lighting the surrounding landscape.

Laughing could be heard coming from the direction of the two lunatics. The glowing red woman suddenly stopped, and a red hand emerged from her. It pushed her opponent back through the door. The glowing red woman flew towards Seth at an alarming speed with a visible red strand leading from her arm to the opposite side of the door through which she had just pushed her opponent. Seth barely saw her move and she was already standing next to him.

"Why haven't you gone through the door? I already told you which one you needed!" she demanded.

"What? I thought you were trying to kill me!"

Jacqui seemed to be struggling. The red string of plasma trailing through the open door moved in unison with her grunts as she explained to Seth:

"I did not, although I would have if Heidi were not stopping me. She was just trying to help you by pointing you to the right door."

"Wait, you are Jacquelyn?" This was extremely confusing for Seth.

The red plasma strand trailing from her heaved violently, then thickened slightly. Jacqui looked at Seth seriously and continued her explanation.

"Look, when you arrived here you met Heidi. She was pretending to be me because she wants to keep you confused — that way you don't know which one of us you can trust. If you want to get to the bridge you will need help from *both* of us, but you will need to pass through many of these doors. Every time either of us goes through one, our polarity reverses. So if I let Heidi back through this door, I will become a sadistic bitch and Heidi will have to try to stop me from killing you."

Seth looked at the glowing red lady.

"So *you're* Jacqui?"

Jacquelyn rolled her eyes.

"Yes, but call me Jacquelyn. Heidi just said that so you would annoy me, which you are doing by not going through that door. It gets harder and harder to trick me into punching Heidi back out the door."

Seth had his hand on the door handle, but he turned to Jacquelyn.

"So, who's going to help me through the next door?"

"The one who isn't trying to kill you," Jacquelyn answered curtly. Seth gave her a suspicious look and walked through the door, hoping he was putting his trust in the right maniac.

The round black handle turned in Seth's hand as he had opened the portal to the next world. Seth saw a much more cheerful looking world; this landscape had emerald green grass stretching for kilometres. Seth could hear birds squawking as they flew through a cloudless blue sky. On the grass stood a plethora of doors, stretching out across the green landscape. In the distance were black-green mountains, reaching up to touch the sky. Seth heard movement nearby. He stood ready to blast the crazy woman — Jacquelyn *or* Heidi — with a jet of white-hot fire. A door just behind Seth opened and one of the two sisters poked her head through to look at him.

"Seth, you need to come through this door," said the sister. Then it looked like she was pulled away by a force on the other side of the door — most likely her twin sister.

Seth faced the door through which he had just been beckoned, then walked towards it and looked through. He saw what looked like another section of The Wandering Cross. A long corridor extended in front of Seth, with walls made of huge mud bricks like the structure he had seen initially. Of course, there were once again all different sorts of doors filling up the space inside the massive corridor. It was possible that Heidi was the one who had called him through the door, in which case he shouldn't listen to her... or maybe he should? Seth thought he understood what was going on with these two spasmodic ladies, but he had not seen either one for about thirty seconds. They both could have flown through several doors in that time, changing which one was helpful and which one was out for his blood. He realised keeping track of the two sisters was going to be paramount to his survival.

Once again Jacquelyn or Heidi shoved their head through the same doorway and yelled for Seth to come through. He took one step forward, when Jacquelyn came fast as lighting through the door he had used to enter this grassy land. She started laughing maniacally and raised both her hands above her head. A blue ball of energy began to gather between them. If this was the sister who was just with Seth in the black landscape, then she must have turned evil after crossing through the door, so it was the good one who had been calling Seth. He jumped through the door from which Heidi had been calling him. He was indeed back in The Wandering Cross, but the woman waiting there did not seem happy to see him.

She looked at Seth, then at the ground and shook her head while she was talking.

"Seth, the one who just came through the door is now trying to kill you, correct?"

From the tone of her voice Seth was sure he was about to hear how he had done something wrong.

"Yes, that's how I knew you were Jacquelyn — no, Heidi, but the good Heidi," he answered. Heidi had stopped shaking her head and looking at the ground, but her flat, condescending tone hadn't changed when she spoke.

"Now I am, but not when I was calling you through this door. This is not where you need to be. You have to go back."

Both of Seth's eyebrows raised as he realised his mistake.

"But evil Jacqui is there! And why did she come through the door if she knew she was going to start attacking me anyway?" he replied. Heidi sighed in exasperation.

"She did it so you would know which one of us to trust, but we need to go back. You just need a head start so I don't kill you, Seth. Now go!"

This is too confusing, Seth thought. It didn't seem like that big a ruse, but Heidi's method of introducing herself as Jacquelyn was very cunning and had thrown him completely. Seth jumped through the door, ready for an onslaught of energy beams. Jacquelyn was still holding a ball of blue plasma above her head. Seth decided avoiding Jacqui's ball of destruction entirely was the best approach. He kicked his foot against the ground as he flung himself quickly upwards. He heard an explosion close behind him and saw that he had taken flight just in time.

From where Seth floated in the air, he could see Jacquelyn flying towards him, blue lightning trailing behind her. Instead of fire, this time Seth sent a rapidly growing root of blue stone towards

Jacquelyn. Jacquelyn dodged the stone beam easily and swung her arm around, bringing her trail of blue lightning forward like a whip. A wall of stone materialised around Seth as he protected himself from the oncoming whip of plasma. All that Jacquelyn could see was a marbled orb falling through the sky as the lightning bounced harmlessly off the non-conductive material. Inside the falling orb, Seth was panicking. He was only about five hundred metres from the ground, so he needed to act quickly or he would be smashed against the walls of his stone barrier as it collided with the ground.

The feeling of weightlessness as he fell was reminiscent of the small room that had transported Seth around the Reference Centre in Chos Garren. He was instantly reminded of his ability to shrink, and he began reducing his size rapidly, effectively increasing the distance between him and the walls of his falling stone prison. Seth's downward momentum kept him floating inside the two metre wide ball as it fell. The **thunk** as it hit the ground shook Seth around violently and he needed to manipulate the air flow around him to stabilise. Slowly, he increased his size again. Seth could hear laughing coming from outside the stone wall. No doubt Jacquelyn was under the impression he had become a red paste inside the orb.

A loud crack boomed across the grass as Seth fired a beam of metal upwards, smashing open the ball of blue stone. It grew twenty metres tall before it stopped. The metallic pole tipped over and crushed several doors into the ground, sending bits of wooden debris flying through the air. When enough dust had cleared, Seth saw Jacquelyn, floating in the air still laughing. Then she stopped suddenly, blinked a few times and burst into an even more intense fit of laughter.

"Is being one foot tall supposed to intimidate me?" Jacquelyn yelled through uncontrollable howls.

Seth looked down at himself and saw nothing strange, then to his surroundings. The doors that had once been normal size towered about ten metres above him; he was not even *close* to his original size. Seth focused on growing, but instead of returning to normal size he shot up rapidly to stand two hundred metres tall.

"No, but this is!" and he was surprised by how loud his voice had become.

Seth's massive fist reached out to grab Jacquelyn but she quickly flew out of the way. Overconfidence came with such height and Seth tried to reach for her once again, even faster. He closed his gargantuan hand around Jacquelyn, leaving a tiny empty space in his hand so she wouldn't be crushed like a mosquito, just a small red stain in his hand. He could feel her pushing against his fingers It stung a bit now and then. Seth laughed: Jacquelyn's screaming reached his massive ears as a small peep, while his laughter boomed across the landscape of doors.

Below Seth, Heidi had crossed through the door and become the evil sister. She saw his enormous foot in front of her and fired a burning red beam from her hand up towards Seth's colossal head. Seth felt the stinging of the beam and looked down to find the source. He saw the slight movement of Heidi and realised that the evil sister was now below him, while the good one was trapped inside his hand. His hand unfolded and Jacquelyn stood in his palm saying something, but Seth could barely hear it. He lifted her towards his ear.

"Gross, your ear is disgusting Seth — but either way, this is an impressive power! I didn't think you would be powerful enough make it to the bridge, but now I am doubting myself. Now! You need to go to the right door," said Jacquelyn as she stared into the maw of Seth's ear canal. "You will need to shrink down again so you can fit through it when I show you which one."

Seth did not like this idea. It would leave him vulnerable to Heidi's attacks which had come to a suspiciously sudden halt. He scanned the ground beneath him and saw no sign of the second sister. The air was silent and static. Seth could see from his current height just how many doors there were; reaching the bridge would definitely be impossible without Heidi and Jacquelyn.

"What would happen if I killed your sister?" Seth asked in a booming voice. Jacquelyn was still on Seth's palm nearby his ear.

"The next time I cross through a door, I would disappear and I wouldn't help you anymore because you would have killed my sister." The tone in Jacquelyn's voice was one of complete seriousness.

This was going to be a difficult journey. At this size, Seth could not fit through any door, but to become small enough to fit through any of them meant he would be vulnerable to one of Heidi's many powers. Seth felt a stinging on his forehead and looked up to see Heidi floating in front of him at eye level. She was extending a red beam to just above Seth's eye. He felt it moving down towards his eyeball and dodged out of the way, accidentally dropping Jacquelyn. He looked around frantically to see where the good sister had gone, and saw the red beam again in his peripheral vision. Seth turned to find where it was coming from. A metal root grew from Seth's outstretched right palm. Heidi could not get out of the way in time and was pushed back by the huge mass of metal.

The giant column of metal fell to the ground with a crash, demolishing at least five hundred doors in the process, while others were pushed backwards by the enormous force. At his current size, the beam of metal Seth had created was about one kilometre long and seventy metres in diameter. He hoped that he hadn't destroyed the door he would need to reach the bridge, and once again scolded himself about how he should really think these things through.

"This is not somewhere I want to be —," Seth heard Jacquelyn's high-pitched voice in his ear; she must have been right at the entrance to his ear canal, "— but she won't realise

FALLEN WORLD

I'm here. You have to stop her going through any doors or I will become evil and I could easily liquefy your brains from here!"

Seth quickly scanned the landscape and saw a black speck flying through the air. When it was close enough, Seth grabbed Heidi and held her in his hand as he had Jacquelyn.

Seth tried whispering so only Jacquelyn would be able to hear but he was sure his enormous voice box would not allow for such subtlety:

"OK, I have her."

Jacquelyn was actually floating nearby Seth's ear canal. There was no way she would stand in the waxy hairs guarding the entrance to his ear drum.

"Good! You know, this would be much easier if you could sit on *my* shoulder instead," she said. Seth's lips stretched into a smile as he realised that he could easily execute Jacquelyn's idea. He could shrink himself so small that she could just walk through the correct door with Seth, and Heidi would have no idea — although Heidi would be the one he needed after Jacquelyn's crossing reversed the sisters' polarity again.

His one hand that wasn't currently being used as a jail for a sadistic element binder gave a thumbs up. He moved it around slightly to make sure Jacquelyn would see. He heard Jacquelyn give an affirmative response in his ear and he started to shrink, realising simultaneously that would mean the release of evil Heidi. As Seth's hand grew smaller, gaps appeared between his fingers and Heidi darted to freedom. Seth was not sure where Heidi had gone but now she was free she would surely notice he was shrinking and becoming more vulnerable.

Jacquelyn was currently about the same size as one of Seth's fingers. A massive shaft of lightning smashed through the air, frying small dust particles in its wake as it barreled towards Seth. Jacquelyn intercepted the bolt, blocking it with a huge shield of invisible energy. A booming sound filled the air as the crack of the thunder reached Seth and Jacquelyn. Still shrinking, Seth watched the lightning bouncing off the transparent barrier and split into smaller streams before trailing off. Keeping track of who was Jacquelyn and who was Heidi, was now extremely important; if Seth hitchhiked on the wrong sister, it would most vlikely spell death. Right now it was quite easy to see who was who, but when Seth was small enough to perch himself on the shelf of Jacquelyn's earlobe, it might be more difficult. He kept his eye on the sister fending off the barrage of electricity and flew towards her, now roughly the same size as her.

Moving towards Jacquelyn and shrinking simultaneously gave Seth the impression that she was moving at an incredibly rapid speed. He jerked back mid-flight, thinking he was preventing himself from colliding with Jacquelyn, but then he quickly realised what had happened. Seth was about level with Jacquelyn's waist now, and he was slightly smaller than a fly. The sizzling of the electricity being fanned out by Jacquelyn's invisible shield sounded like thunder when it reached Seth's microscopic ears. He quickly ascended towards Jacquelyn's head. The folds in her clothing looked like small mountains and the stains that seemed subtle in reality looked like huge lakes of filth at this magnification. The pale pink landscape below Seth became a blur as he accelerated his approach to Jacquelyn's ear, his eyes were watering slightly from the wind resistance.

A few seconds later, Seth was staring into Jacquelyn's hairy ear canal, each strand of hair covered in a lumpy film of yellow wax. The scene was extremely poorly lit, but there was clearly a humongous mass of wax that Seth would take extra care to avoid behind the hairs. He shouted into her ear, making sure he would be heard. Jacquelyn's massive head jerked away violently.

"Not so loud Seth, you're right next to my eardrum!" Jacquelyn said in a deep rumbling voice as she moved her head slowly back to its original position. From Seth's angle, all he could see was the waxy and hairy entrance to Jacquelyn's eardrum coming straight towards him at high velocity, Seth desperately flew away, letting out a short yelp but catching himself short before he caused Jacquelyn more hearing damage. Seth did not see the smile appear on Jacquelyn's face.

"I told you it was gross!"

"I'm in position. If you head to the next door, I'll be riding with you" said Seth calmly into Jacquelyn's ear.

Jacquelyn fired a bright pink bolt of electricity against the flow of white lightning coming from Heidi's attack. It seemed to knock Heidi's attack away effortlessly, and Seth gripped Jacquelyn's earlobe tightly as he felt the acceleration of her flight push him backwards. The doors on the ground became a blur as they zipped past. Seth was grateful that the hunk of metal he fabricated earlier hadn't destroyed the target door; he was curious how many strange and dangerous destinations he had blocked off. Jacquelyn stopped suddenly, almost sending Seth flying. He angrily told Jacquelyn to give him a bit of warning next time, and she replied that they had arrived at their destination door.

"You will have to get off my ear as soon as we are through. I am not the same person when I pass through the aperture, but I retain the same memories. In fact, you will be better off flying through the door before me." Jacquelyn's resonating voice rattled in Seth's head, but he understood and agreed with her plan.

Seth spoke his last words into Jacquelyn's ear before flying through the now-open door:

"I will see you on the other side, or Heidi."

On the other side of the door Seth could see a flat, deep-blue landscape dotted with thousands of doors. He flew through the door but remained in miniature form, hoping to elude the evil sister if she was the one who came through next. A gargantuan bolt of lightning shot past Seth, bringing a deafening crack with it. Quickly, Seth ascended to be out of the direct pathway of the door. He scrambled to figure out a method of determining which of the sisters would come through the door next. He thought that if both of the sisters were aware of their bipolar nature, then the evil sister who was now Heidi would not come through the doorway, as she knew that she would become good-Heidi and point Seth in the correct direction. Jacquelyn, however, should not want to come through either, since she would also be aware that the moment she did, she would become sadistic-Jacquelyn and try to kill him. Jacquelyn was the one who knew about Seth's current size situation, so the best person to come through now would be Heidi, and Jacquelyn knew this. If good-Heidi came through, then Seth wouldn't need to stay microscopic, and if evil-Jacquelyn emerged Seth would be safer if he was back at normal size, or even bigger. Seth returned to his normal size and waited, listening to the fierce exchange of energy blasts on the other side of the aperture.

FALLEN WORLD

Chapter 14

The landscape behind this door had surprised Seth. At first glance, it looked like a perpetual ocean, stretching as far as the eye could see but the water was completely static. The surface of the gigantic ocean had been frozen in place; waves were in the middle of breaking when some incredible force had drained all heat from the water and suspended it mid flow. The blue of the water beneath could still be seen through the transparent icy surface. Seth watched the mist flowing from his mouth condense as it floated away. He could feel the chill of the surrounding air and was glad he was still wearing his trusty robe. He had positioned himself slightly above and behind the door he had used to enter, and watched the area he expected (well, hoped) good-Heidi would first appear, should she enter this realm. Movement beneath the ice caught Seth's eye. He saw a multitude of small, coloured objects darting back and forth. He looked around to see if there were more but they all seemed to be focused around the area where he was now floating. Apparently Seth's presence had attracted whatever these things were.

Suddenly the small shapes dispersed and only a solid blue colour could be seen again. The dark blue of the water trapped beneath the ice looked like it had a darker patch just beneath Seth now. He squinted to see if he was correct — and the patch became darker and bigger. Seth looked up hastily, expecting to see something falling towards him, but only a cloudy grey sky was visible. The patch was now about ten metres in diameter and growing faster, Seth realised it must be something *beneath* the ice, and he quickly flew upwards to avoid whatever was now swimming towards him. He rose high above the jagged, frozen surface of the ocean, and could now see the shape of the creature more clearly. Again, Seth squinted downwards. More light reached the creature now, revealing a dark brown colour with two black patches that looked like they might be eyes.

The creature came into focus for a split second just before it smashed through the surface of the ice. In that same instant, Seth had observed that the creature also possessed a mouth about the same width as its head, now revealed to be 25 metres wide. Its mouth was slightly open before it pulverized the ice, revealing countless teeth that looked sharp enough to slice Seth in half effortlessly. Even if they were at all dull, their size and crushing power would have had no trouble killing him. The cold water splashed up in front of the creature as it emerged from its ocean habitat. Massive shards of ice turned white as their smooth surface was ruined by the reckless beast smashing upwards. Some shards were flying towards Seth but most flew off harmlessly to the side. Seth felt the cold spray and flew even higher, fearing the creature would be able to launch itself to his altitude.
He looked down he as flew upwards. Out of the white explosion of water emerged the creature. Its mouth was now completely open; obviously, it had come to the surface to feed. Bouncing around inside the huge monster's mouth were many doors breaking in half with splinters flying everywhere. In the creature's mouth Seth could see the door through which he had arrived along with many others and began to panic. If that door was destroyed, would he be trapped in this frozen place? Would Heidi or Jacquelyn be able to enter this world to help him find the bridge of The Wandering Cross (a journey he was now really starting to consider whether or not it was worth the trouble)?

The skin of the beast now flying towards Seth was shiny with water. The creature was a teardrop in shape, with the bulk of its mass angled towards Seth and the pointed end flailing about behind it. The huge mouth of the beast divided its two pigmentations; the top half was a dark, speckled brown, where its shiny black eyes stared menacingly towards Seth. Underneath its mouth, what must have been the belly of the substantial beast was a pallid fleshy tone. It had two long tendrils of that same colour, each one extending from either corner of its mouth and trailing metres beyond its body, waving in the wind as it charged towards Seth.

The ascent of the beast slowed as it began to reach the apex of its trajectory. Seth was glad he had flown higher, or he would now be taking the first step in the epic journey of being digested. The creature's mouth snapped shut, still ten metres below where Seth was now floating. Seth heard the crunching of wood as the doors inside its gaping maw were crushed, and with them, his only certain chance for egress. Seth could hear the loud swallowing noise coming from the aquatic animal just as it was about to succumb to gravity. Suddenly the head of the beast exploded, and Seth felt the mist of the liquefied viscera splash against his exposed skin. The warmth of the disgusting fluid dripping from him was sickening. The space where the beast's head had just been was now occupied by the two sisters, shooting beams of fire, lightning, and plasma in all directions as they struggled to incapacitate each other.

Instead of just Heidi or Jacquelyn coming by herself through the aperture as Seth had hoped, it was Heidi and Jacquelyn simultaneously, which made the problem of keeping track of them even more difficult. Seth stared at the two sisters as they tumbled through the air, an entire spectrum of colour spraying in all directions. Seth needed to quickly dodge a few beams that flew towards him. His movement caught one of the girl's eyes and she started to shout to Seth.

"You need to go that way Seth!" shouted one of the sisters — hopefully the good one — and she fired a straight blue-white beam. Seth understood and immediately began flying in the direction she had indicated. Then the other sister shouted to him.

"No! Seth! That's Heidi! You need to go this way!" and a perfectly straight bright pink beam fired into the depths of the ocean.

Seth tumbled through the air as he attempted to change directions too quickly. His robe slapped him in the face and blocked his vision. Without any sense now of which way was up, Seth had no idea how he should be manipulating the airflow around him. He pulled away the corner of the robe clinging to his face and saw the frozen ground getting closer and closer. He fired a blast of air at the approaching surface and bounced back upwards. Cracks appeared in the ice and spread outwards in a chain reaction, snaking out to fill a large radius with white fissures. The cracking of the ice slowed. Chunks of ice fell loose and sank slightly.

Now the two sisters were both acting as if they wanted to help; clearly this was another trick to deceive Seth, and unfortunately, an extremely effective one. The arrival of both sisters at the same time had made it impossible to determine which was which. The path the second sister had indicated lead into the depths of the ocean, so that was definitely the least appealing. Seth was inclined to follow the first path, which seemed to lead over the top of all the other doors. It seemed less likely there was anything lurking there as he followed its path into the clouds with his eyes. The two sisters were still fighting and both beams lighting his two possibilities had disappeared.

Jacquelyn and Heidi were floating fifty metres above the icy surface of this world, staring at each other from a distance. Small discharges of energy arced from their bodies randomly and ignited the air around them. The sister closest to Seth turned around and looked straight at where he was floating, about fifty metres away.

"Seth listen: that is Heidi," she shouted, pointing to the other sister. "You need to go down there!" and another bright pink beam of plasma fired straight down into the ocean, steam appearing where it penetrated the water's surface.
The other sister yelled at her counterpart:
"Stop leading him to death, Heidi! Why would there be a door under the water?!" She fired a blue beam of lightning at the other sister.
The sister that had just fired a beam into the water dodged out of the path of the blue lightning and continued flying towards the frozen tundra. She stopped, put her hand on one of the doors, and looked back. Seth heard the other sister shout "NO!" and realised what was happening. The good sister – Jacquelyn or Heidi – knew going through the door would turn the evil sister good, and the good sister remaining on this side of the door would then indicate the same direction: into the ocean. Through the door went the sister, and sure enough, the remaining sister fired a beam into the ocean, only this one was a pale blue.
"Yes Seth, I am Heidi. Into the ocean with you!" she shouted, flying in the direction she had just indicated.
Seth followed her into the ocean. Not knowing how deep he would have to go, Seth created a bubble of air around himself just before he entered the water. It was about three metres in diameter; Seth hoped the oxygen inside would last him long enough to reach the right door. It was easy to see Heidi as she had created a bubble of air around herself much larger than his, creating an obvious, highlighted circle of a lighter blue. However, the deeper they went, the darker it all became. Seth sped up a little and entered Heidi's bubble of oxygen. She had just created a small glowing orb that floated above her hand, illuminating the surrounding seascape.
"How deep is it?" Seth asked her.

He noticed there were small silhouettes moving behind the surface of the surrounding ball of oxygen. Heidi stopped and turned around so Seth could catch up.

"It's pretty deep. It won't take long to get there, but we need to hurry up. Jacquelyn went through the door to one of the chaotic space dimensions, so we don't have much time before she finds her way back here," Heidi responded in a calmer repose than Seth was feeling.

As Heidi was talking Seth noticed much larger silhouettes were also moving in the water behind her. He needed to ask.

"What about those huge things, do we need to worry about them?"

Heidi smiled slightly and shook her head. She raised a hand and a yellow ball flew into the water, rippling the surface slightly and disappearing almost instantly. The water surrounding the entry point of the projectile turned a slight red colour.

Heidi lowered her arm after mercilessly killing the beast on the other side of the water barrier.

"Come on Seth," she said, and started heading deeper in a slightly different direction. Seth really wanted this underwater journey to end soon. He was unnerved by her callous actions, but he needed to focus on finding the door and getting out of this water prison. Seth had never seen so much water, nor had he had ever been so deep underwater that there was no sign of the sun anymore. This entire experience was actually quite formidable to him. The idea that the bubble of oxygen might collapse and he would suddenly be overcome by billions of litres of water made him want to leave this world as soon as possible. Hopefully the next one would be a little more hospitable.

Heidi looked back over her shoulder as she spoke to him.

"I think the door may have moved with the currents." Her eyes quickly glanced at something behind Seth and she continued to speak. Instinctively, Seth spun around to see what Heidi had spotted, expecting one of those massive creatures heading towards him, Instead, it was a light in the distance with a small silhouette behind it. Seth could just make out the outline of what looked like one of the sisters behind the approaching light source.

Oh no! Seth thought, and saw the surface of bubble in front of him lose cohesion as it fell towards him. Inside Seth was a level of fear he had never experienced before. It caused a tingling sensation that washed over him like a six ton wave.

"NOOOOO!" Seth screamed, and he frantically created a ball of air to push the water away from him where it could never get him.

Suddenly the ambient noise of water disappeared. Seth had had his eyes closed when he pushed the water away. He opened them to a very big surprise: the water that could have dragged him to an icy doom a few seconds ago was now kilometres away. In his frightened state, his power had increased to such a monumental level that the ball of oxygen surrounding him grew so big it broke through the surface of the ice, merging with the atmosphere of above the water world. The sun was now illuminating his surroundings and Seth looked around. Above him, what must have been Jacquelyn was just a small speck in the distance, and beneath him Heidi had surely been pushed deeper into the water. The light didn't reach that far, and he could not see her. Another speck was visible about five hundred metres below him. It seemed rectangular from this distance, but Seth wasn't sure. The sphere carved out by Seth's sudden expansion of air began to lose its perfect shape. He realised that the water was no longer being held up by the air and that this four kilometre-wide orb would soon be filled with water again. That rectangular shape was most likely the door he needed, so Seth pushed himself in its direction with the surrounding air.

He had that tingling feeling again as he saw the water crashing towards him from every side. The wind was making his eyes

FALLEN WORLD

water as he approached the door, but he could fly much faster than the water could fall so he was not panicking too much. Soon Seth had his hand on the door; he still had a little time before the water would reach him so he looked around to see if Jacquelyn was nearby. He didn't want to lose track of the sister's identities and polarities again.

Jacquelyn was actually only seconds from reaching Seth when he saw her.

"Go Seth!" she shouted.

The combination of the approaching torrent of water and Jacquelyn's encouragement were more than enough motivation for Seth to stop thinking and just go through the door. He pulled it open and saw a dark landscape with glowing green shapes moving around. He jumped through.

Seth looked around: this world had an eerie, calm feeling to it. The landscape was mainly grass or dirt, although it was hard to tell where one ended and the other began since everything was so poorly lit. There were sources of light from different creatures moving around, but all very slowly. Every creature produced a fluorescent green light which did not travel very far, but cast an ambient light over their surroundings. The most common creature that Seth could see moving about was a huge kind of worm. It was made up of segments divided by thin sharp lines and moved along the ground like a legless caterpillar, arching its back and bringing its rear half forwards, then extending its body straight again to push its front half forwards. It seemed a very inefficient manner of travelling, but then again, without any limbs it was most likely the creature's best option.

Seth felt a human-sized object slam into his back and his feet left the ground as the momentum pushed him forward. He landed roughly and skidded across the grass, pulling himself upwards with the surrounding air to avoid any serious injuries. He turned around to see which of the sisters had just collided with him before admitting how pointless it was. Since the one closest behind him in the previous world was good-Jacquelyn, this must mean that evil-Jacquelyn had just knocked Seth several metres through the air. She was now facing Seth and raising her arm, no doubt to project some kind of deadly energy at him. So far, Seth didn't have any good method of stopping their attacks; his blast of sparks was possible, but watching the sisters fight showed Seth how much stronger than him they both were.

Before she could fire anything at Seth, a wall of stone encased Jacquelyn. The wall formed a thick dome, blocking any evidence Jacquelyn was there. Just as fast, the rock dome shattered, sending fragments of heavy stone flying in every direction. Seth flew higher to avoid the flying shrapnel — and to put some distance between himself and the sadistic woman. He looked back to see Heidi come flying through the door and smash into Jacquelyn, causing a small shockwave. Jacquelyn was now the good sister. Seth believed he now had some idea of which one was which. He wanted to help; another stone dome appeared, significantly thicker than the last one Seth had manifested. This time, it was to trap Heidi. He expected the dome to explode just as quickly as the last one, but instead a powerful torrent of water came bursting through the still-open door behind her, engulfing the dome and much of the landscape. Jacquelyn moved towards Seth, shouting "GO!"

Seth was not certain where he should go. Again she shouted it, and still Seth did not know where to go.

"Grow! Seth, you need to grow!" Jacquelyn yelled at him. She was now close enough that her words had become discernible above the thrashing of the water below.

So Seth grew again. It happened so quickly that his huge feet slammed into the ground, creating footprints several storeys deep. He stopped his growth at about two hundred and fifty metres tall. All of the gigantic worms now appeared regular in size, while the rest of the glowing green animals had been reduced down to indistinguishable specks of light.

He heard Jacquelyn's voice in his ear.

"Not much further to go Seth. I've noticed the objects you materialise at this size are proportionally humongous, so when you see me fire a beam at her, try creating that ball of stone around her again. It will be a pink beam, just so you don't encase the wrong sister."

"OK." Seth's voice echoed, causing some of the creatures on the surface below him to briefly luminesce even brighter.

Seth stood still as he kept his eye out for a pink beam. He saw a white ball of energy appear in the distance and start growing rapidly, and sure enough a straight pink beam shot out from behind him towards the figure below the growing white plasma sphere. Seth created a globe of stone around Heidi and watched as it drifted towards the ground. The wall of this ball must have been about twenty metres thick; despite Heidi's powerful nature, Seth did not expect her to break through it easily. It made a solid thud as it hit the ground, along with the crunching noise as some of the doors squashed beneath it.

"Do it again!" Seth heard Jacquelyn's voice echoing in his gigantic ear canal.

He created another sphere around the sphere, adding twenty more metres of stone between him and Heidi.

"Again!" Jacquelyn shouted in urgency causing Seth to jerk his head away slightly from the sharp noise.

Another layer of stone appeared around the previous two. Before Jacquelyn could cause more hearing damage, Seth materialised another layer, this time of metal, then another stone layer and finally, another metal layer. There must have been about one hundred metres of solid stone and metal surrounding Heidi now; it wouldn't hold her back forever but it would definitely buy some time. Seth shrank himself back down to his normal size. The stone dome he had just created towered above them menacingly, but they could speak to each other normally now. Jacquelyn was smiling.

"I am impressed Seth. You did not look like the kind of person that would even get through the second door, but you actually helped me subdue Heidi to go through the last door," she said.

Hearing that there was only one door left made Seth feel a hundred times lighter. It hadn't been a long journey time-wise to get to this final blue-green world, but it certainly felt like it. Seth had almost died several times and would be glad to be out of constant danger and confusion.

"Great," he said. "I think I have had enough of your dual nature. No offence Jacquelyn, but dealing with you two is exhausting."

Jacquelyn laughed before she responded.

"It's perfectly alright Seth, I understand. It's not supposed to be easy to get to the bridge of The Wandering Cross. This path was only supposed to be passable for Faust and Trikala, which makes it even more impressive that you made it this far. But we need to get away from here now; the door is in that direction," and Jacquelyn pointed towards some hills. They seemed to host more giant glowing worms than the surrounding environment.

"But we are travelling on a different heading at first so Heidi can't find us so easily when she escapes. Come on Seth, one more door to go!" Jacquelyn beckoned to Seth as she flew away. Seth followed her.

***

Jacquelyn led Seth a few kilometres away from the huge dome before she changed direction to head towards their destination, the next door.

"We've come far enough now Seth. She'll be waiting at the aperture but at least she won't stop us on the way to it," Jacquelyn said as Seth floated after her.

He decided to take this opportunity to ask some of the questions that had been weighing on him.

"So, what kind of ship is The Wandering Cross? You said it's not like others."

Once again Jacquelyn's laugh preceded her answer.

"It's ironic Seth, that you are fighting so hard to reach the bridge, but you don't even know what sort of power it has to offer. No one besides Faust or Trikala has made it this far before."

"Well, I believe it holds knowledge — knowledge that will help me get back home. I have been trying but I am not powerful enough to find Swevender, nor reach it if I do," Seth responded, a little defensively.

Jacquelyn stopped and turned around to face him

"Seth, this ship will bring you further than you can imagine. To use it to travel back home would be a huge waste of its potential.... when you are at the bridge you will understand."

Seth was staring at Jacquelyn, trying to formulate a response, but she turned around and pressed forward before he had found the appropriate one.

"Yeah, alright," he muttered to himself as he followed her.

Jacquelyn began talking over her shoulder to Seth once he had caught up with her again.

"So Seth, how is it that you are able to 'manipulate matter'?" She emphasised the words, showing how unaccustomed she was with the term. "I've never heard of anyone who wasn't a manifestation of Faust or Trikala that could do it."

Seth increased his speed a little to bring himself alongside Jacquelyn before he responded.

"I had never heard of Faust or Trikala when I was taught 'water wielding' at school. Where I'm from, everybody learns the basics as they grow up. It is a big part of our society. It is basically matter manipulation, but only using water. We were raised believing that using any other kind of matter ran the risk of destroying the world."

Jacquelyn once again laughed at a private joke to which Seth was not privy.

"It has a greater danger than that: you could end up destroying the universe. Well, turning it inside out, really, but you wouldn't feel that effect since you would also have turned inside out. Actually, using water is an even bigger risk."

Seth knew Jacquelyn wanted him to ask why, but he would rather finish his story than give her the satisfaction of hearing her own voice again. He continued, a bit louder than necessary:

"So we thought we would destroy the world if we tried any other matter than water."

"Ha! And now it is destroyed! Probably by Faust and Trikala too!" Jacquelyn interrupted. Seth's irritation was clear on his face as he attempted to tell his story for a third time.

"And, well yes, the world was destroyed, along with my home," Seth said. "I landed on the surface of the world and somehow was pulled into the Restyard, where Jacobus and Iselle sent their familiars when they were finished with them."

Jacquelyn opened her mouth to interrupt and Seth became extremely annoyed. She hesitated

"What?!" Seth shouted.

"I just think Jacobus and Iselle were actually Faust and Trikala, that's all," said Jacquelyn almost giggling at Seth's frustration.

"OK," Seth replied, hoping that she was done for now. "Well, one of the familiars hadn't fallen into his eternal sleep

FALLEN WORLD

yet, so he used our time in the Restyard to teach me the principles of element binding."

"Yes, *that's* what it's called," Jacquelyn said automatically. Then her eyes popped open wider and she looked at Seth. "Sorry, I did not mean to interrupt you again."

"It's OK, I've finished anyway. The familiar Red taught me a lot." Seth said in a monotone voice, realising that this was going to be a very one-sided conversation.

Jacquelyn smiled broadly.

"Well, it's interesting that Jacobus and Iselle taught you to only use water..."

Seth spoke again, relishing the opportunity to interrupt Jacquelyn.

"They weren't the ones who taught us; it was three water wielders, Io, Kern and Marsa."

"Still probably Faust and Trikala, although I don't know who the third one is. Water is made up of stuff from another universe though," Jacquelyn said. "Strange of them to teach an entire world that using water is safer than other matter, when the opposite is true."

"What do you mean exactly?" asked Seth.

Jacquelyn took a deep breath, indicating she was about to begin a lengthy recitation.

"Well, as you should know, the world is made up of smaller particles —"

"Atoms," Seth said, skilfully hiding just how proud he was of knowing this.

Jacquelyn continued.

"Correct, and inside each atom is another universe — in fact the same universe, but inverted. This means every atom inside an inverted universe carries an energy charge inversely proportional to the mirror atom in this universe."

Seth looked suitably astonished. He thought what the Inquirer had told him in Chos Garren was overwhelming, but Seth had the idea this conversation would be even more astonishing.

"OK, there are universes inside each atom. This I knew already..."

Jacquelyn sighed.

"Yes, but there are even more universes than that," she said dismissively, "and when you drain an atom of its energy you increase the tension on its connection to this universe. Atoms are all connected to the edge of the universe by a hollow pathway. Whenever you take energy from an atom — for example, when performing 'matter manipulation' — you put strain on its connection to the edge of the universe. This string connecting the atom to the universe's edge hasn't yet been observed, but this is part of an idea called 'string theory'. It explains the reason for gravity and the hidden connection between many objects throughout the universe.

There is a point when an atom's 'string' cannot be stretched anymore, and the atom's shape is unfolded. It becomes part of the wall of our universe, and the entire universe turns inside out around the atom. The point where the atom's wall is indistinguishable from the wall of its universe is called the 'reflection point'; everything inside the atom becomes our universe and is inverted as it passes that point. It becomes what it was reflecting: *our* universe." Seth's head was spinning. Maybe it wasn't the temple that contained knowledge, but the sisters guarding it...

Jacquelyn continued with her disconcerting explanation.

"The atom itself does not get inverted but instead physically changes place with its counterpart in the inverse universe, so it gains back all of the energy it once had. Remember, in the inverse universe its energy was increasing while in ours it was decreasing. This could be happening right now Seth; your body is made from atoms too, and you would not

even notice it happening. But, to bring you back to my point: water contains one atom from another universe, and two from this universe. Using this matter for manipulation means you are pulling on two different universes at the same time. I don't think even Trikala or Faust knows what this kind of interaction this could cause... This might explain why they created your world."
Seth had come to terms with the fact he would not understand what Jacquelyn was talking about.

"No... Io, Kern and Marsa did not create a whole world. I come from a city with only three thousand residents."
Jacquelyn looked at Seth with surprise in her eyes.

"Wow! That is an extremely discreet operation, no wonder I have never met anyone like you. This explains how you displaced thirty cubic kilometres of water; you clearly have an affinity with it. You are an interesting guy Seth. I hope you never meet Faust and Trikala."
She had said this with fondness in her voice — yet she was hoping for him never to meet the only two people who might be able to help him get home. Seth was confused.

"Uhh, why not?"
Jacquelyn looked at him.

"Seth, I and my sister are a creation of those two. Do you think we are a friendly pair?"

"Well, yes and no," Seth said.
Jacquelyn laughed.

"Very funny Seth, but honestly: would you want to encounter us again?"
Seth yielded.

"No, not really."

"That's what I thought. Well we are not even close to the worst things they have created, and to them, you and the rest of all of the universes are *insignificant*. They think of themselves as gods, and to be honest, they are not far from it, but the multiverse has yet to be completely explored. For them, anything they haven't encountered yet is just an opportunity to learn something new to become even more powerful. Believe me, meeting them is one of the worst things you could ever do."

"Oh." Seth did not have much to say to that. Jacquelyn seemed genuine and he certainly did not know enough to argue with her.

Now Jacquelyn looked at Seth with an easy grin, suggesting some sort of joke was coming.

"Are you ready Seth? This will actually be an easy door compared to the other ones. The only person that needs to go through the door is you. No need to worry about bringing the right sister with you; once you have entered the bridge, the game is over."

Seth was unsure what exactly would happen and opened his mouth to ask, but he was distracted as a pulse of blue energy bounced off an invisible barrier less than a metre in front of him.

They had reached the final door. Similar to the last one underneath the icy ocean, it stood solitary, no field of doors where a thousand dangerous mistakes could be made. Heidi had already opened fire, but luckily Jacquelyn was paying attention, and unlike Seth, she was ready to deflect the oncoming energy assault. Heidi was glowing a fluorescent blue, arcs of energy branching off into the air so bright that Seth could see more afterglow than darkness when he closed his eyes. Jacquelyn shot from Seth's side and tackled Heidi away from the door.

Seth saw his opportunity and flung himself forward. He grabbed the handle and opened the door. He moved to cross the last threshold and finally enter the bridge — but then he saw panels and buttons very much resembling the Inquirer's technology and hesitated. He looked at Jacquelyn, who was currently deflecting a bright pink beam of plasma. It streamed around the edges of her energy shield and annihilated the blue-green landscape behind her.

Seth stepped through the door. Jacquelyn, or Heidi, quickly came through the door behind him and smashed Seth up against a wall of buttons. They both stood up. Seth rubbed his head where it had collided with the console and saw blood on his hand as he pulled it away from his face. The other sister stepped calmly through the still open door onto the bridge. Seth was ready for an onslaught as the first sister turned evil, but both sisters remained amicable this time. He looked at one of them, one eyebrow raised questioningly.

"It's OK now Seth. The last door only changes negative polarity into positive — well from your perspective it does. We are both here to help you operate The Wandering Cross now," Jacquelyn said to Seth.

Heidi smiled and spoke too.

"Yes Seth, you don't need to worry about us anymore. Now, where do you want to go?"

Seth felt a little relieved, and overwhelmed. He had just travelled through a terrifyingly dangerous labyrinth where he had almost died countless times. He had no idea where this ship could even take him and he would rather relax a little bit before having to explore again. The interior of the bridge was similar to the hollow sphere he had seen before entering any of the doors. The walls he had seen elsewhere in The Wandering Cross were made of humongous khaki-coloured bricks; these ones, however, seemed less dilapidated and had no evidence of cracks. Inside the sphere there were silver and black consoles everywhere. There was a small cage in the corner that could fit a standing human inside it. The floor of the bridge was just below the halfway point of the sphere. It was a matte silver and completely spotless, like no one had ever actually walked over it. The grey and black consoles looked less modern than the Inquirer's technology; a lot of the buttons were raised squares and circles, mainly red and green in colour. Some of the buttons seemed to be illuminated, while the majority were not. The roof of the bridge was about five metres from the ground and a lot of the consoles followed the shape of the sphere. Some were so far up it seemed impossible that anyone could reach them.

The design of the bridge was a little underwhelming, really. Seth expected to have his mind blown by multidimensional devices and visions of worlds he did not understand, similar to his experience in the Restyard. But he had either experienced so much now that he was not as easily impressed anymore — or it was just not an impressive design. Heidi saw Seth's reaction.

"Trikala and Faust did not care much about aesthetics; practicality was their main concern. You still have not told us where you want to go..."

Seth looked at Heidi, then Jacquelyn, then back to Heidi.

"Well, where can this ship take me? I just want to go home to be honest."

Heidi frowned and was the first to speak:

"Why would you do that? We are in a ship that literally moves through universes — and you don't even want to leave your own atmosphere?"

"Where's your sense of adventure, Seth?" asked Jacquelyn.

"I would not be here without a sense of adventure, I have adventure coming out my backside at this point!"

Jacquelyn wrinkled her nose in disgust.

"Why would it be coming out of there?"

"You think any of those worlds that we just travelled through were impressive? I guarantee this is several steps up from anything you've seen," Heidi added.

"I still kind of just want to go home. I think I already have enough stories for now"

Jacquelyn smiled slightly.

FALLEN WORLD

"You will regret it; the stories that will come from this can't even be told."

"Well, what good is that?" Seth demanded.

Heidi spoke again:

"It strengthens your soul, the very source of your powers. The reason my sister and I are so strong is because of our experiences; all the things we learn teach us impossibilities to strive for. You won't get that by just going home. You were taught element binding to tip the power in this universe, and many others, but you can't reach that point unless you actually travel to those other universes."

Seth began scratching his chin, thinking about the possibility.

"To go to an entire other universe... that's something I never really imagined... but I can still go home afterwards, right?"

Jacquelyn and Heidi looked at each other, both with mischievous grins. They moved to separate consoles and began pressing buttons. They occasionally waved their hands at the consoles in the ceiling of the bridge and buttons moved and illuminated above them.

Seth had no idea what was happening. He looked at the walls of the bridge and they seemed to be moving. The consoles were also moving slightly, rearranging themselves. A strange brown liquid dripped onto Seth's hand. He looked at it as the droplet sprang upwards and rejoined the brick from which it came. Seth noticed now that his hand was becoming more... *liquid* than usual. In fact, the entire bridge had gained a much more fluid texture than usual. Jacquelyn spoke, her voice was extremely dampened but Seth could understand her perfectly.

"Relax Seth, this is completely normal."

Everything was melting, dripping, and the small droplets would somehow migrate back to their original forms, maintaining their original mass and shape.

"We have arrived! Let's take a look outside," Heidi proudly proclaimed. She opened the door that had brought all three of them into the bridge.

Instead of the glowing green and blue landscape with gigantic worms, Seth saw a world made up of viscous liquids, constantly moving and being rearranged by unknown forces. Some of it leaked through the door and into the bridge. Seth moved forward, but as he raised his foot to advance, part of it remained attached to the floor. Before he could put his foot back down, the rest of it had snapped into the dripping mass of what must be his leg, and made it whole again. Seth looked at the door framing the melting landscape, then at his hands as they dripped to the floor and reformed themselves. He hoped this next adventure would teach him to start thinking ahead and stepped through the doorway.

Made in the USA
Middletown, DE
27 March 2019